Happy Birthday

MURDER

BONZAI
MOON

BonzaiMoon Books LLC
Houston, Texas
www.bonzaimoonbooks.com

1

Beanie glanced at his wife, contemplating the question she'd just asked him.

In the fading sunlight casting rays across the pergola, the love of his life was still the prettiest woman he'd ever seen with her perfect cheekbones, delicate features, and her hair pulled back in an artfully constructed messy bun.

Picking up the bottle of ginger beer from the small table next to his chair, Beanie took a sip. Keeping a watchful eye on his young sons, four-year-old Ethan, and two-year-old Evan, he enjoyed the balmy breeze, dark lavender sky, and relaxing time with the family he was grateful for and blessed to have.

They'd had an early supper of goat tenders and steamed veggies, which Noelle coaxed the boys into eating by promising them ice cream and an hour of playtime in the backyard before bath time. As Noelle shepherded the boys out of the kitchen, Beanie grabbed two ginger beers from the fridge. Outside, Ethan and Evan ran around, squealing, and laughing, playing some sort of game, a mash-up of hide and go seek and cops and robbers. Beanie joined Noelle under the pergola, taking a seat on one of the pastel-painted Adirondack chairs arranged in a semi-circle.

"Roland …" prompted Noelle.

Beanie sighed. "How do I feel about turning thirty?"

Noelle looked at him. "You upset about it? Okay with it? Do you care?"

"Doesn't bother me," said Beanie. "Figured it would happen one day."

Smiling, Noelle asked, "So you're still okay with the thirtieth birthday party?"

"Yeah, I can't wait," said Beanie. "But ..."

"But what?"

Beanie hesitated. When his wife had suggested a party to celebrate the thirtieth birthday for him and his fraternal twin sister, Robyn, Beanie had thought it was a great idea. Normally, he and his twin didn't get to spend their birthdays together. Robyn usually took a girls' trip and Beanie had an intimate dinner with Noelle.

But thirty was a milestone birthday, one that should be a big deal.

Robyn wasn't convinced. His sister believed thirty was a millstone. She didn't like the idea of no longer being twenty-nine.

"Robyn might not be able to make it," said Beanie.

"Why not?" asked Noelle. "Does she have other plans?"

Beanie took another sip of ginger beer. "Not exactly."

"What does that mean?"

"She's upset because she's turning thirty," said Beanie. "She thought she would be married with kids by now. I told her she would find somebody, and he would be the love of her life, but I don't think she believed me."

Noelle frowned. "Wait. I thought she already found somebody. Are things not going well between her and Henry?"

Beanie said, "Things are ..."

"What?"

"Robyn said things are fine," said Beanie, rubbing his jaw.

"Just fine?" questioned Noelle. "I thought things were getting serious between them."

"So did I ..." admitted Beanie. "But now I'm not so sure."

"But they're living together," said Noelle. "That seems pretty serious to me."

"Robyn said she and Henry are serious enough," said Beanie. "And don't ask me what that means because she didn't elaborate."

Beanie recalled the last conversation he'd had with his sister about her love life. A few days ago, they'd met for lunch in Pourciau Square. Over goat stew from the popular Loco Goat food truck, Beanie's favorite, his sister confessed her worries.

But it turned out that turning thirty was the least of her fears.

Robyn had hinted at problems in her relationship with Dr. Henry Montague, the guy his sister had been dating for the past three months.

Seven months ago, Robyn had been accepted into a Forensic Nursing program taught at St. Killian University. During the year-long program, his sister had taken a temporary assignment as a Surgical RN at St. Killian General Hospital. The move from St. Basil, where she resided, facilitated the need for temporary residence.

Initially, Robyn had contemplated rooming with their parents, but she didn't want to be treated like a teenager, having to adhere to a curfew and being questioned about her whereabouts.

Beanie offered her the extra bedroom in the modest, modern Oyster Farms home he shared with Noelle and the boys, but Robyn had demurred. She loved her nephews, but the rambunctious boys could be a handful, and wouldn't give their favorite auntie a moment's peace. A colleague at the hospital had told Robyn that a cardiac surgeon named Dr. Montague had a room for rent in his townhouse located in Adagio Bay, a ritzy, upper-class enclave.

Robyn rented the room, and a month later, she and Henry were dating.

Beanie glanced at his wife. "Between you and me ... I don't think things are working out with Henry. I don't think she trusts the guy."

"Has he given her a reason not to trust him?"

Clearing his throat, Beanie took another sip of his ginger beer as he struggled to come up with an answer.

When Robyn had confided her reservations about Henry, she'd sworn him to keep the information private.

Specifically, she'd told him not to tell Noelle.

It was no secret that his wife and his sister were not fond of each other, and that was putting it mildly. Robyn had never really warmed up to Noelle. When Beanie had first introduced them, Robyn was polite but standoffish, and later declared that something about Noelle seemed shady. When Robyn learned about Noelle's former affiliation with the PC-5, a dangerous island cartel, she felt her suspicions had been validated.

Finding out that his wife had once pledged allegiance to the cartel had shaken Beanie to his core and might have ruined their marriage, but they'd committed to working through their issues. Beanie was upset that Noelle had kept secrets from him, but he was more hurt that he'd created an environment where she didn't feel as though she could trust him with the shame of her past. He hated knowing his wife feared he would judge her, then divorce her and prevent her from being a mother to their boys.

"Roland …" prompted Noelle.

Beanie focused on his boys who were digging in the dirt near the row of hibiscus bushes along the back fence. Indecision gripped him. He didn't want to lie to his wife. But, neither did he want to be disloyal to his sister.

"Robyn didn't want to go into details," said Beanie. "I just hope she ends things with the guy if he's not right for her."

"If she doesn't trust him, she should just confront him," advised Noelle.

"Confront him?"

"Like you confronted me," said Noelle. "You had your suspicions and doubts and—"

"That's not true," said Beanie. "I didn't confront you."

Noelle stared at him.

Beanie didn't back down. "I came home and found you with bruises all over your face. I asked you what happened, and you started telling me how you didn't deserve me and the kids. And I asked why you were saying those things and you told me."

Looking away, Noelle took a sip of ginger beer.

"Babe, listen," said Beanie, hoping to avoid a painful trip down memory lane. "I don't—"

"Mommy! Mommy!" Ethan ran up to Noelle with his hands behind his back. "I have something for you!"

"You do?" Noelle put her bottle down and stretched out her arms, smiling at Ethan. "Oh, you're so sweet! What is it? Let me see!"

Beanie snickered, recognizing the mischievous gleam in his son's warm brown eyes. Noelle was probably expecting a Hibiscus flower, plucked from the bush. Beanie suspected his oldest was harboring something creepy and crawly. A bug. Or maybe a frog.

"Look, Mommy!" Ethan opened his hand. "I got a lizard for you!"

Screaming, Noelle jumped up and made a mad dash toward the back door that led into the kitchen. "Don't come near me with that thing! Get it away!"

"Don't be scared of the lizard, Mommy!" said Ethan, holding the squirming, slithering animal by its tail.

"Ethan!" censured Beanie, but his tone lacked the discipline required to convince Ethan that he'd done something wrong. Beanie didn't think a lizard—one of God's creatures living in its natural environment—should cause Ethan much trouble. He had to be a disciplinarian even though he thought Ethan's "gift" was funny.

"Mommy doesn't like lizards, remember?"

"Why not?" asked Ethan. "The lizard won't hurt Mommy! He wants to be her friend!"

"Lizard is Mommy's friend!" chorused Evan, who toddled up to Beanie, his little chubby legs churning as he climbed onto Beanie's lap.

"Lizard is *not* Mommy's friend," called Noelle from the corner near the back door, where she cowered.

Containing his laughter, Beanie said, "Ethan, you know I think the lizard probably has a family that he wants to be with. So why don't you take him back where you found him, okay?"

Frowning, Ethan said, "But the lizard doesn't have a family, Daddy. That's why he wants to be in our family."

"Lizard is family!" echoed Evan, clapping his hands. "I want lizard!"

Impressed by his four-year-old's logic, Beanie said, "How do you know the lizard doesn't have a family?"

"I can tell the lizard is lonely, Daddy," said Ethan, trying to pet the lizard, which wriggled frantically.

"Ethan, the lizard isn't lonely," said Beanie. "He's probably just lost. Take him back where you got him."

Lower lip protruding, Ethan shook his head. "But, Daddy—"

"Ethan," said Beanie, hoping his tone brooked no further protests.

Scowling, Ethan said, "Okay, fine, Daddy, but the lizard is gonna be sad!"

"Sad lizard," said Evan, trying to crawl down from Beanie's lap to follow his brother.

"Stay with me, buddy," said Beanie, tightening his hold on Evan.

Ethan ran to the rear of the backyard. Noelle returned to her chair and was waiting for him when he came running back.

"Here Mommy," said Ethan, presenting Noelle with a vibrant pink hibiscus flower.

Taking the flower, Noelle hugged Ethan, pulling him into her arms.

Evan rested his head on Beanie's shoulder, and Beanie gave Ethan a quick thumbs-up, which the little tyke acknowledged with a wink.

As the sun set, and the boys quieted down, Beanie was grateful for his family and hopeful that Robyn would work through her issues with Henry. He wanted his sister to find the right guy, start a family, and enjoy precious moments like this.

2

At four o'clock in the afternoon, a balmy breeze scented with the fragrance of the sea wafted through the air as forty or so of Beanie and Robyn's family members, close friends, and co-workers congregated in the backyard. Eating, drinking, dancing, and making merry, they celebrated the thirtieth birthday of Beanie and his sister Robyn.

For the past two hours, Beanie and Robyn had worked the crowd, mixing and mingling, raising a glass whenever someone proposed a toast, sharing a laugh, and reminiscing about old times.

As a lively Soca beat blasted from speakers hidden near the trunks of several Palm trees, Beanie ambled over toward two colleagues from the *Palmchat Gazette*, fellow reporters Stevie Bishop and Sophie Carter.

"So how's it feel to be over the hill?" asked Stevie, laughing.

"Ha, ha …" said Beanie, shaking his head. "I'll let you know when I get over it."

"If you get over it," said Sophie, smiling. "You might trip and fall."

"And tumble down to the bottom," said Stevie, continuing the joking narrative.

"And who'll be there to help you get up?" asked Sophie, cackling.

"Funny. Funny," said Beanie, taking it all in stride. "You guys got jokes now, but just you wait."

"It's going to be eight years before I'm thirty," announced Sophie, her tone smug.

Beanie said, "Trust me, those eight years are going to fly by faster than you think!"

Excusing himself from Stevie and Sophie, Beanie weaved through the guests, stopping to chat with a group of high school friends who congregated near the buffet table.

"Living fossil!" one of the guys hollered out, grabbing Beanie into a fierce bear hug as the other men roared with laughter.

"You're next!" said Beanie, laughing as he pointed to the men. After enduring several minutes of good-natured joshing, Beanie moved on, heading toward some friends from church sitting at one of the benches. He was having a great time. The turnout had been fantastic—not too many people, but enough to make things lively and interesting. The weather was wonderful, but he hadn't been worried. The music was perfect, the food was perfect, and the atmosphere was festive and carefree.

Still, he did have cause for concern.

Strolling toward the bench, beer in hand, Beanie glanced around, catching the eye of loved ones, and giving a wave to acquaintances. He was looking for Robyn.

His sister had been drinking a lot, more than usual. Beanie had observed her doing shots with every person who asked. Earlier, when he'd pulled her to the side and cautioned her to pace herself, she'd scowled at him, accusing him of trying to ruin her mood.

Beanie had protested. "Just don't want you to puke all over the yard and I'll have to clean it up."

Rolling her eyes, Robyn said, "I know how to hold my liquor, little brother. And I told you, once I do thirty shots, one for every year I've been alive on this earth, then I'll switch to water for the rest of the night. Satisfied?"

Beanie would have been more satisfied to know she was chasing each shot with an eight-ounce glass of water, but his sister was an adult. And he didn't want to spoil her fun, since she seemed to be having a good time. At least, when she was with her friends from high school and her work friends. Robyn seemed less jovial when Henry was around. The handsome doctor wasn't clingy. He seemed more than happy to let Robyn mingle while he sat in one of the pastel-colored Adirondack chairs, drinking a beer and checking his phone.

Now and then, however, Robyn brought a friend or family member to meet Henry. In those moments, his sister appeared distant and stiff, though she smiled. Once, Beanie saw his sister and Henry at the buffet table, with their arms around each other's waists, but they seemed to be posturing, pretending to be a loving couple. Or, maybe not pretending, thought Beanie, deciding to give his sister and her boyfriend the benefit of the doubt. Maybe they were trying to be a loving couple. Trying to make their relationship work.

Beanie was suspicious and worried.

Deciding not to dwell on his concerns, Beanie continued toward the bench. Halfway there, he spotted Noelle and Robyn standing near the buffet table with three other guests, talking to a group of Beanie's cousins.

Catching his wife's eye, Beanie smiled.

Noelle looked fantastic in a coral-colored, strapless sundress. Sometimes, Beanie couldn't believe Noelle had chosen him. He'd been told he was a nice-looking guy, and he'd never had problems with women, but his wife was beyond gorgeous. Often, people told her she was a dead ringer for the supermodel Naomi Campbell.

His wife blew him a kiss, then waved her arm, beckoning him to come to them. Beanie strode to the buffet table, where he was introduced to Robyn's friends from St. Killian General Hospital—Nurse Sara Parker, Dr. Emily Taylor, who went by Mimi, and her fiancé, Tim.

"Well, little brother!" yelled Robyn, her sing-song voice laced with intoxication as she grabbed him and slipped an arm around his waist. "How does it feel to be thirty?"

"Doesn't feel much different than being twenty-nine," said Beanie, steadying his sister as she swayed against him and cackled a bit too loudly at his deadpan answer.

"So, wait, Robyn, you're the oldest?" asked Tim, pushing his black-rimmed Harry Potter glasses up his nose.

"Duh, Tim," said Sara. "You heard Robbie call him her little brother."

Shrugging, Tim gave a sheepish smile. "Oh, yeah, she did say that. So how much older are you?"

"Older enough," said Robyn, still swaying as she rested her head on Beanie's shoulder. "But you wouldn't know it because little brother acts like he's my dad!"

"That is not true," protested Beanie.

"Beanie doesn't want me to have any fun," said Robyn, though her voice was full of inebriated mirth. "He's a husband and a father so he's much more mature than I am!"

"You'll be an old married lady, soon, girl," said Sara.

"I don't know about that," quipped Robyn.

Mimi waved a hand dismissively. "Sara's right. You know Henry's going to propose."

"Maybe he will," acknowledged Robyn.

"Do I hear wedding bells?" asked Noelle, smiling.

Beanie felt something within him revolt at the idea of Robyn marrying Henry. He wanted his sister to be happy, but he wasn't convinced Henry was the right man for her.

"Honey check your ears," Robyn said to Noelle. "That's Soca you hear."

Annoyed by his sister's unnecessary rudeness, Beanie glanced at Noelle. His wife's smile faltered a bit, but Beanie knew she wouldn't let Robyn ruin her mood. His wife had been through a lot, and she could handle a salty sister-in-law. Beanie still planned to give his sister a few choice words.

Robyn said, "Anyway, even if Henry asks, doesn't mean I'll say yes."

"Why wouldn't you?" asked Tim.

"Ohmigod! I love this song!" announced Robyn, grabbing her friends, and pulling them toward the makeshift dancefloor—the porch beneath the pergola. Moments later, dancing suggestively, Robyn raised her arms and swayed them back and forth. She cackled as her friends encouraged her to drop it like it was hot and show them what she was working with—which his sister seemed eager to do.

"Go, Robyn! Go Robyn!" chorused the partygoers on the porch, forming a circle around her.

Shaking his head, Beanie chuckled at his sister's antics.

Noelle walked over to him.

"Having fun?" asked Noelle.

Beanie slipped an arm around Noelle. Guiding her to a semi-private spot near a Palm tree, he said, "I'm having a great time."

"Robyn seems to be having a good time, too," said Noelle as a loud, euphoric shout erupted from the dancefloor.

"Maybe too much of a good time," said Beanie, watching as Robyn danced with two guys, grinding her hips as they sandwiched her.

Noelle frowned at him. "How old are you?"

"What?" asked Beanie, confused.

"Thought you were thirty, not eighty," teased Noelle. "Stop sounding like a crotchety old man."

"That was my protective brother voice," said Beanie.

Noelle gave him a light punch in the arm. "Speaking of that. Want to hear my nagging wife voice?"

Beanie made a face. "Not really."

"Can you call Tricia and make sure the boys are okay?" asked Noelle.

"And while I'm checking on our kids," began Beanie, "what are you going to be doing?"

"Dancing to this song," said Noelle, swinging her hips as she sashayed toward the porch.

3

Minutes later, in the bedroom he shared with Noelle, Beanie used the house phone to call the babysitter, Tricia, the niece of a friend from their church.

"The boys are playing with my puppy," said Tricia.

"Everything going okay?" asked Beanie, hoping the boys wouldn't return home demanding a canine. Dogs were a huge responsibility, and while he planned to buy a pup for the kids in the future, he thought they were a bit too young now.

"Going great!" said Tricia. "We went to the beach and the park and then to the library."

"The library?"

"Had to get a few books to read at bedtime tonight."

Beanie felt a strange hitch in his chest. The bedtime story routine was one he and Noelle performed automatically. Often, he wasn't in the mood to read two or three books to Ethan, but he didn't like the idea of someone else doing what he considered "daddy duty". He missed his little guys like crazy and hated that he wouldn't be able to tuck them in and kiss them goodnight.

After hanging up with Tricia, Beanie forced himself to shake off the melancholy. The boys were only spending one night with Tricia. He and Noelle would pick up Ethan and Evan tomorrow morning and tomorrow night, he'd be wishing that Evan would stop splashing water and that Ethan would fall asleep after just one story.

Resolved to continue having a great time at his birthday blowout bash, Beanie left the bedroom. Heading down the hallway, he passed the boys' room. After a glance into the dark room, he continued, but then stopped. Beanie frowned. Had he seen something in the boys' room? No, not something. Someone. Slowly, Beanie turned and took a few steps toward the boys' bedroom.

Voices floated into the hallway. Beanie paused, listening. The voices rose and fell. The sentences were hushed, clipped, and curt, as though the whispered words were forced through gritted teeth.

Beanie took another step closer to the opened doorway.

"… calm down, okay?"

"I am not calming down!"

"Robyn, please—"

"Tell me why she is still calling you?" asked Robyn. "And don't try to lie and pretend she didn't call because I know she did!"

"She probably wanted to talk about a patient."

"Stop lying!" hissed Robyn. "She's an OB-GYN. You're a cardiologist. She wasn't calling about a patient."

"I don't know why she's calling, okay?" responded Henry. "I told you, she's crazy. She doesn't want to accept that we're not together anymore and I've moved on."

"Well, you need to make her accept it!" Robyn said.

"Look, I have tried, okay?" said Henry. "But … you have to understand. She has deep feelings for me, and …"

"And what?"

Riveted by the clandestine conversation, Beanie wondered who Robyn and Henry were talking about. An ex-lover, most likely. But who was the woman? And why wouldn't she stop calling Henry? Why couldn't she accept that Henry had moved on? And why had his sister chosen to get involved with a guy who had a clingy, possessive ex?

Henry said, "And I didn't want to tell you this, but …"

"You didn't want to tell me what?"

"She has a history of instability," said Henry.

Beanie frowned, his worry increasing. A past girlfriend who couldn't get over being dumped was annoying, but not necessarily a cause for concern. However, a former girlfriend who was unstable could be problematic.

"A history of instability?" echoed Robyn. "What does that mean?"

"I had to get a restraining order a few months before we broke up," said Henry. "She was stalking me, and ..."

"And?" Robyn's voice rose. "Tell me!"

"She tried to kill me."

A jolt passed through Beanie.

"Oh my God ..." whispered Robyn. "Are you serious?"

"As serious as the gun she held to my head," said Henry.

"Is that why she's calling?" asked Robyn. "Is she threatening you again?"

Beanie wanted to know the answer, as well. More than that, he wanted his sister as far away as possible from a guy with a dangerous, gun-wielding ex-girlfriend.

"She has said some ... disturbing things," said Henry.

"What kind of disturbing things?" demanded Robyn. "What does that mean?"

"Look, don't worry, okay?"

"Don't worry?" scoffed Robyn. "How can I not worry? You tell me your psycho ex tried to kill you and you tell me not to worry?"

"There's no need to worry because I have protection," said Henry. "I bought a gun."

"You bought a gun?"

"It's in the nightstand on my side of the bed," said Henry.

"And you're really going to shoot her with it?" asked Robyn, her voice laced with incredulity.

"If she tries to hurt us," Henry insisted.

"You need to call the police," said Robyn. "Get another restraining order."

"I don't want to do that."

"If you won't do it, then I will!

"Robyn, wait a minute," said Henry. "You can't—"

"Get your hands off me!" Robyn seethed. "Don't touch me!"

At that moment, Beanie had heard enough. Stomping into the boys' room, he flipped the switch on the wall near the door, flooding the room with bright light.

"Roland!" Robyn's eyes widened as she stared at him, looking like the proverbial deer caught in headlights.

Beanie looked at Henry. The good doctor glared at him with narrowed eyes.

"What are you doing in here?" Robyn demanded.

"I could ask you the same question," said Beanie. "What's going on?"

Shaking her head, Robyn said, "Nothing. We were just talking."

Remaining silent, Henry stared at Robyn.

Beanie said, "I want to talk to my sister. Alone."

After Henry left, Beanie closed the bedroom door.

Robyn rolled her eyes. "Why did you close the door?"

"I don't want Henry listening to our conversation," said Beanie.

"Oh, you don't want him eavesdropping on me and you like you were eavesdropping on me and him?"

"I can eavesdrop if I want to in my own house," Beanie told her. "Now what is going on with you two?"

Arms folded, Robyn snipped, "Nothing."

"Don't tell me nothing," said Beanie. "Who's the psycho ex who tried to kill Henry?"

"Wow, you really were listening to everything we said, huh?"

"Tell me," said Beanie.

"Her name is Dr. Elizabeth Adams," said Robyn. "She's an OB-GYN at St. Killian General."

"An unstable gynecologist who pulled a gun on a man who filed a restraining order against her," said Beanie, disturbed by the idea of a crazed woman delivering children.

Robyn rolled her eyes. "If that's even true …"

"You don't believe Henry?" asked Beanie. "You think he was lying to you?"

"I don't know …" Robyn shook her head. "But if he is lying, it certainly wouldn't be the first time. He's been doing a lot of lying these past few weeks."

"Elaborate, please," said Beanie.

Robyn sighed. "A few weeks ago, I thought Henry was cheating on me with Liz. So, I started following him."

"Did you catch him with her?"

Robyn shook her head. "No, but I caught him with a man."

Beanie was shocked. "A man?"

"No, I don't mean like that," clarified Robyn. "I mean … it was a guy I've never seen before. I was in my car, watching from a distance. The guy was wearing a hoodie and sunglasses, I think. Anyway, Henry had left the hospital at lunch to meet with this man at a scuzzy bar in Little Turkey. The Fish-Eyed Fool."

Beanie burst out laughing.

Robyn glared at him.

Struggling to contain his mirth, Beanie said, "Never been there."

"Consider yourself lucky," quipped Robyn. "It's the kind of place the guidebooks advise you to stay away from."

"You have any idea what they were meeting about?"

"No, but it seemed pretty intense," said Robyn. "The conversation seemed very confrontational. Very aggressive."

"Did you confront Henry about the guy?"

"He claimed the guy was an old friend he owed some money," said Robyn. "Money he doesn't have right now. He said the guy was hassling him about paying the money back."

"Hassling him?"

"Threatening him," said Robyn.

"Interesting," murmured Beanie under his breath. He wouldn't have guessed that the cardiac surgeon had money problems. In addition to his duties at St. Killian General Hospital, Henry was also a partner in a cardiac specialty center in the Aerie Islands. The ritzy heart clinic catered to CEOs and rock stars and Middle Eastern royalty.

"I didn't believe Henry's story about the guy," said Robyn. "I knew he was lying about owing the guy money."

"How?"

"Because I followed Henry a few more times," said Robyn. "He met this guy again at the Fish Eyed Fool—"

Beanie laughed out loud again.

Robyn glowered at him. "What is your problem?"

"The Fish-Eyed Fool?" Beanie shook his head. "You don't think that's funny … um, guess you don't."

"Are you finished laughing?" asked Robyn. "Can I finish telling you how I knew Henry was lying to me?"

Beanie cleared his throat. "Sorry. Go ahead. I'm listening."

"One of the times when Henry met the guy," said Robyn, "they had a drink and then the guy pulled an envelope from the front pocket of his hoodie. Henry took the envelope and put it in the inside pocket of his blazer."

"An envelope?"

"A thick envelope," said Robyn, giving him a knowing look.

"What do you think was in it?" asked Beanie, though he suspected he knew the answer.

Robyn rolled her eyes. "You know, for an investigative reporter who's supposed to have all these inductive reasoning skills, you can be pretty dense sometimes."

"As an investigative reporter, I speculate and extrapolate but I never assume when I don't have all the facts," countered Beanie.

Robyn said, "It was an envelope full of cash. After Henry met with the guy," said Robyn, "he went to the Pourciau Bank. I saw him pull out a fat stack and hand it to the teller."

"Did you confront Henry?"

"Why would I do that?" asked Robyn. "So he could lie to me again?"

"Why do you think he's lying about the gun he bought for protection?" asked Beanie.

"Because tonight is the first I've heard about the gun," said Robyn. "He just brings it up out of the blue when I tell him to file another restraining order against Liz. He doesn't want to get the cops involved. Why? Because he's got a bullet with Liz's name on it? Yeah, right. Henry couldn't shoot the broad side of a barn to save his life."

"So why do you think he bought the gun?"

"I have no idea," said Robyn. "For all I know, there is no gun."

"You can check the nightstand and find out," suggested Beanie.

"Or, I can just drop it," said Robyn, "and stop acting like a suspicious, jealous girlfriend. I can stop being a doubting, distrustful woman. Things have been going well with Henry and I don't want to ruin the relationship over petty foolishness."

"Dishonesty is not the same as petty foolishness," said Beanie, surprised by his sister's whiplash one-hundred-eighty-degree attitude. "You need to trust your gut. Henry has already lied to you."

"Everybody lies, Roland." Robyn jumped up, paced toward the window, then pivoted to face him. "You know that better than I do … "

Beanie decided to ignore his sister's not-so-subtle dig at his wife.

Robyn said, "No one is completely honest all the time and I don't want to throw away my chance at happiness if there's no reason to!"

"But it sounds like there is a reason," said Beanie. "Henry's been acting shady. It's not just the phone calls from his ex, but it's also the money that sketchy guy gave him."

"That could have been a legitimate business transaction," said Robyn. "And just because the guy was wearing a hoodie doesn't mean he's sketchy."

Beanie exhaled. "Robyn, are you sure Henry's the guy who's going to make you happy?"

"Did you know that Noelle was the woman who would make you happy when you met her?" demanded Robyn. "No. And yet, you were willing to take a chance and get to know her and see what could happen. Now, you have a beautiful family. I just want the same opportunity."

"I want that opportunity for you, too," said Beanie. "And I know you'll get it. But I want you to have it with the right guy. A man who'll truly honor and cherish and love you."

"Can we just go back to the party?" Robyn asked, heading toward the door.

Beanie stopped in front of his sister, blocking her progress. "I'm not sure, from what you've told me, that Henry is the right guy for you."

"And I don't think a woman whose father used to kill people is the right woman for you," Robyn shot back. "A woman who sold drugs for the PC-5—"

"Stop trying to deflect from the issue we're talking about," Beanie told her.

"I'm not trying to deflect," insisted Robyn. "I'm just trying to point out that we both have problems with each other's partners, okay? Henry's not perfect, but neither is Noelle. And you still love her. You still want me to give her a chance."

"Which you don't," said Beanie.

Robyn threw up her hands. "Because I can't. You could have been killed because of her lies. And not the PC-5 lies, the lies about that pharmacy student."

"You're deflecting again," warned Beanie, fed up with his sister's evasive attitude.

"No, I'm not deflecting," said Robyn, stepping around him. "Right now, I'm leaving."

4

"Speech! Speech! Speech!" chorused the guests crowded around the buffet table, where a large three-tiered cake had been placed.

Holding a flute of champagne, Beanie glanced around at his family and friends, smiling, holding flutes of their own, waiting expectantly for poignant words of wisdom. Beanie forced himself to smile although he no longer felt festive or jovial.

Standing next to him, Robyn held a flute by the stem as she smiled.

Beanie could tell his sister was struggling to maintain her grin, as well.

As twins, they were uniquely tuned to each other's emotions. Beanie knew Robyn was still upset because they'd argued about Henry. Beanie was still angry, even though the heated exchange had taken place almost an hour ago. He'd tried to push their terse words from his mind, but he wanted to shake some sense into his sister. He couldn't understand why his sister was willing to stay with the smug doctor, who stood at the front of the crowd, standing next to Noelle. Grinning broadly, Henry appeared confident and relaxed. Beanie wanted to slug the smug jerk.

But he couldn't hit Henry. At least not at the present moment.

He had to give his guests what they wanted. Clearing his throat, Beanie said, "Okay, okay. I'm not exactly great at speeches or speaking in public, and I'm going to need a second, so as they say, age before beauty."

Robyn gave him a light punch in the arm as the guests whistled, clapped, and shouted out good-natured jibs and jeers.

"Well, first of all, I want to thank my sister-in-law, Noelle, for throwing this party," began Robyn, her words garnering thunderous applause from their friends and family.

Catching his wife's gaze, Beanie blew his beautiful, beaming wife a kiss as she basked in the accolades.

"At first, I wasn't too sure about celebrating my thirtieth birthday in such a grand, lavish way," admitted Robyn, "but this party has been so wonderful and I've had such a great time, so thank you again, Noelle. You've made turning thirty a lot less painful than I thought it would be."

After more clapping and laughter, Robyn went on. "And now, to my little brother. We started this journey together … and I'm so glad that we've always been together and had each other's backs … it's been great growing up with you, and of course, we don't always see eye to eye—"

"That's an understatement," quipped Beanie, feeling some of his ire dissipate as the guests chuckled.

"But I know you're always on my side," said Robyn. "You're my best friend, Roland. I love you forever."

As the guests cheered, raising their glasses, Beanie hugged his sister. His heart warmed by her loving sentiments, he held his sister tightly, resolved to forget about their disagreement.

Pulling away from Robyn, Beanie took a sip of champagne, and then said, "So, now that I've had some time to get my thoughts together—"

"It's about time!" called out a friend.

Another yelled, "Took you long enough!"

"This better be good, Beanie!"

"No pressure, little brother," teased Robyn as the chuckling died down.

After taking a deep breath, Beanie said, "Ditto to everything my big sis said—"

"Aw, man, you can do better than that!" someone said.

Nodding and laughing, Beanie said, "Robyn, you know I love you and you're my best friend."

Applause broke out through the crowd.

Beanie waited for the clapping to cease, and then said, "And out of all the people in the world, you are—"

"The biggest tramp!" The vicious words came from somewhere in the crowd, sending a shockwave of whispered outrage and hushed murmuring among their family and friends. Seconds later, after pushing and shoving through the guests, a woman burst out of the crowd and staggered toward Robyn.

Beanie glanced at his sister. "What is going on?"

Scowling, lips pursed, Robyn stared at the bleary-eyed, dark-haired woman.

Sara broke free from the crowd and marched toward the woman. "What are you doing here?"

"You weren't invited," said Mimi, following Sara.

"Get out of here!" ordered Tim, echoing the sentiments of the other guests, many of whom shouted at the brunette to leave, threatening to do her bodily harm if she didn't.

"I'm not leaving until I toast the birthday girl!" the woman said, her words slightly slurred.

Beanie stepped in front of Robyn, shielding his sister. "I don't know who you are, but—"

"I'll handle this," said Henry, maneuvering through the guests, grabbing the woman's arm, and pulling her away. "You never should have come here."

Trying to yank away from Henry, the woman said, "You and that trollop never should have—"

"Shut up!" Henry forced the woman through the parting crowd.

"You're not going to get away with what you did to me, Henry!" the woman screamed. "I'm gonna make you pay for what you did, you monster!"

Beanie turned to Robyn, who was surrounded by her friends, Mimi, Sara, and Tim, their expressions grim, a mixture of frustration and disgust.

"Who was that?" asked Beanie.

"Henry's psycho ex-girlfriend," said Tim.

"Dr. Liz Adams," said Mimi.

"That was Dr. Liz Adams?" asked Beanie, staring at Robyn, remembering what his sister had told him about the psychotic woman.

"I can't believe she had the gall to crash the party," said Sara, her shrill voice laced with confusion.

"What was she thinking?" asked Mimi.

"Obviously, she wasn't," said Tim.

"How did she know about the party?" asked Noelle.

"She might have heard us talking at work," said Mimi.

Expelling a shaky breath, Robyn said, "I'm going to make sure Henry gets her away from here!"

"You sure that's a good idea?" asked Beanie, but Robyn was already walking away.

"Wait, Robyn," called Mimi. "We'll go with you."

Exhaling, his stomach twisting slightly, Beanie shook his head as his sister hurried to catch up with Henry. As Mimi, Sara, and Tim followed Robyn into the house, Beanie turned to Noelle. "Did that just happen?"

Slipping an arm around his waist, Noelle looked up at him and said, "Let's get you another glass of champagne."

5

Staring at the empty backyard, littered with balloons, streamers, and other party decorations, Beanie smiled as Noelle snuggled next to him, sitting on his lap.

An hour had passed since the thirtieth birthday bash had ended. When the last friends and family members finally said their goodbyes, Beanie and Noelle returned to the backyard. They'd intended to share a private dance beneath the pergola but ended up collapsing in one of the pastel chairs.

Noelle said, "Did you enjoy the party?"

Slipping an arm around his wife, Beanie pulled her closer. "Best birthday ever. I love you so much, babe."

Noelle placed a hand on his cheek. "I love you, too. So much."

Beanie said, "I love you more."

"I love you just as much," said Noelle. "If not more."

Beanie said, "The day I first met you was the best day of my life."

Smiling, Noelle asked, "Even though you had a shellfish allergy."

"I thank God for that allergy," said Beanie. "If my face hadn't swollen up like a blowfish—"

Noelle laughed out loud and gave him a few more kisses.

"—we wouldn't have met," said Beanie. "And I can't imagine not meeting you. Can't imagine my life without you and the boys."

"You'll never have to imagine that," said Noelle.

Beanie exhaled.

"Babe …" Noelle frowned slightly. "Why the long sigh?"

"I was just thinking about Robyn."

"What about her?" asked Noelle. "She had a good time, don't you think? Well, she was having a good time until that crazy woman crashed the party."

"That crazy woman is the least of Robyn's worries."

"What do you mean?"

Beanie said, "I don't know if my sister is in the right frame of mind to make the best decisions for her life."

"Why do you say that?"

"I know my sister wants what we have," said Beanie. "She wants to be in a loving, fulfilling relationship and I want that for her. I want her to find a guy who she can fall in love and start a family with, but I also don't want her to rush into a relationship with the wrong person."

"And by the wrong person, you mean Henry?" Noelle asked.

"He's not the right guy for her." Beanie scoffed. "The guy is shady, Elle."

"Why do you say that?" asked Noelle.

"Earlier, when I went into the house to call Tricia and check on the boys, I caught Robyn and Henry in Ethan and Evan's room," said Beanie, looking at his wife. "They were arguing."

"About what?"

"The crazy ex-girlfriend who crashed the party," said Beanie. "Her name is Dr. Liz Adams. She's a gynecologist at St. Killian General. Robyn thinks Henry and Dr. Adams are fooling around behind her back."

"Does she have proof?"

"Not exactly," said Beanie. "A few weeks ago, Robyn tried to get proof, so she followed Henry."

"Did she catch him with Dr. Adams?

"She caught him with some guy."

"What?"

"I had the same response," said Beanie. "But it's not what you think. The guy gave Henry an envelope full of cash."

"Why? Who is the guy? Does Robyn know?"

"She has no idea who the guy is or why he gave Henry money," said Beanie. "But Henry told her that he owed the guy some money."

"Then why would the guy give Henry money?" asked Noelle. "That doesn't make any sense."

"Right," said Beanie. "That's why Robyn didn't believe Henry's story. But then …"

"Then … what?"

"Then Robyn seemed to change her mind about Henry's story like that." Beanie snapped his fingers. "She goes from not believing Henry to believing him."

"Why would she do that?"

"I think Robyn is accepting Henry's word and ignoring her doubts because she's decided she wants to be with him. So, she's going to rationalize and justify his shady behavior so she can feel comfortable with her decision to stay in a relationship with a guy who's not right for her."

"Babe …" Noelle rested a hand against his cheek. "Doesn't everybody justify the reasons for their decisions?"

Staring at the hibiscus and rose bushes along the back fence, Beanie said, "Yes, but …"

"You know, Robyn feels the same way about me and you as you feel about her and Henry," said Noelle. "She thinks I'm the wrong woman for you and that you rationalize your decision to be with me."

Shaking his head, Beanie said, "I know she feels that way, but it's not the same—"

Beanie's cell phone rang. Startled by the loud chirping, Beanie sat up. As Noelle moved off his lap and into the chair next to him, he retrieved his phone from the pocket of his pants.

"Who is calling at …what time is it?" asked Noelle.

"10:13 …" Glancing at the Caller-ID display, Beanie felt a flurry of apprehension in his chest.

"It's not Tricia, is it?" asked Noelle, panic in her tone. "Oh God, I hope the boys—"

"It's Robyn," said Beanie, answering the phone. "Hello?"

"Roland?" whispered Robyn, tears in her voice. "Are you awake?"

His heart thudding, Beanie asked, "What's the matter?"

"Can you come over?" pleaded Robyn. "I think someone broke into the townhouse …"

6

"Is the person who broke in still in the townhouse?" asked Beanie, his heart pounding so hard, he could feel it in his skull. Flooded with dread, he asked, "Can you sneak out without being seen, or—"

"Did someone break into Robyn's townhouse?" demanded Noelle. "Oh my God! Beanie we need to call the cops!"

Nodding at his wife, Beanie held up a hand.

"No, no, I said I *think* someone broke in the townhouse," clarified Robyn, her tone hurried and hushed. "But I don't know for sure."

Confused and rattled, Beanie said, "I don't understand. Robyn, are you okay? Tell me—"

"Is Robyn okay?" Noelle asked.

"I was sleeping when I heard a noise in the living room," said Robyn. "I thought it was Henry. I called out to him but then I heard more noises and that's when I started to wonder if someone had broken into the house. I yelled that I had a gun, and I would use it and I did."

"What?" Beanie was confused, still rattled with fear for his sister.

"I fired two warning shots," said Robyn. "But I don't think I hit anyone."

Beanie asked, "Are you sure?"

"No, Roland, I'm not sure," snapped Robyn. "I don't even know if someone really broke in."

"What is she saying?" asked Noelle.

Beanie held up a finger, signaling that Noelle should wait.

"Maybe it was just the curtains blowing in front of the patio doors. Henry likes to keep them open at night and sometimes —"

"Wait a minute. Henry likes to keep the patio doors open at night?"

"This is a safe, security-patrolled complex," snapped Robyn. "Lots of our neighbors keep their terrace doors open to take advantage of the sea breeze."

Beanie wasn't exactly relieved. "If it's that safe then why do you think someone broke into the townhouse? Have you called the security patrol, or—"

"I don't want to call the security patrol," said Robyn. "Can't you just come over?"

Beanie asked, "Where is Henry?"

After a pause, Robyn sighed. "He's not here."

"He's not?"

"That's why I called you to come over," snapped Robyn. "If he was home, I wouldn't have—"

"Where is he?"

After an exhale, Robyn said, "He went for a run on the beach."

"A run on the beach?" Beanie asked. "At ten o'clock at night?"

"Roland, can you just come over, please?"

"I'm on my way," said Beanie. "Call the police when I hang up."

"Okay, fine," said Robyn. "Hurry and come over."

As Beanie ended the call, Noelle jumped up.

"What are you doing?" Beanie asked.

"We need to go and make sure Robyn is okay," said Noelle.

"You don't have to come with me," said Beanie, mindful of the animosity between his sister and his wife, which might flare up under the tension of the situation.

"You're not going over there alone," said Noelle. "What if the person who broke in comes back?"

"The cops should be there by the time I show up," said Beanie, rubbing his jaw.

Hands on her hips, Noelle said, "I'm coming with you."

Beanie started to protest but was silenced when Noelle grabbed his hand and started to pull him to his feet.

Moments later, Beanie fished his keys from the bowl on the table in the entryway. He and Noelle hurried out of the house and climbed into the SUV. Leaving Oyster Farms, Beanie headed downtown. After driving through the heart of St. Killian, they reached the road leading to Adagio Bay.

Fifteen minutes later, Beanie clutched the SUV's steering wheel with hands that still trembled slightly. Focused on driving just above the posted speed limit, he tried not to think the worst and concentrated on keeping the road. The last thing he needed was to get into an accident.

"We're almost there," said Noelle.

Startled by his wife's voice, Beanie nodded. He and Noelle hadn't spoken since they'd left the house. Beanie had been too busy trying to ignore the horrible thoughts in his mind. He couldn't imagine anything bad happening to his sister. He didn't know what he would do if—

Stopping the thought before it got out of control, Beanie cleared his throat. "Henry should have been there."

"What?"

Staring at the dark road ahead, a two-lane ribbon of concrete illuminated by his headlights, Beanie said, "My sister should not have been at that townhouse alone. Especially considering that Henry has a crazy ex-girlfriend who tried to kill him, which was why he got a gun. Not to protect my sister, however. To protect himself."

Noelle said, "Robyn didn't tell you where Henry was?"

"I don't think she knows," said Beanie, glancing at his wife. "Still, he shouldn't have left my sister alone. If something happens to Robyn because of him, I will—"

"Beanie!" Noelle yelled. "Watch out!"

Beanie's heart shot into his throat as he whipped his head back toward the road.

Stark bright headlights flashed across a man staggering in the street, inches from the hood of the SUV.

Cursing, Beanie yanked the wheel hard to the right, and slammed on his brakes, praying he wouldn't hit the man as the SUV spun in a circle. As the tires screeched against the pavement, Beanie struggled to control the vehicle as it fishtailed before shuddering to a stop.

"Oh my God!" whispered Noelle.

Beanie turned toward his wife. "Noelle, are you okay? Are you hurt, or—"

"No, no, I'm fine," said Noelle, unbuckling her seatbelt. "I'm okay … but that guy was walking in the middle of the road."

Beanie stared straight ahead through the windshield. The SUV faced a row of luxury yachts. Shocked, Beanie realized the car had spun almost one hundred eighty degrees and now sat horizontally across the two lanes.

"Babe … I think something is wrong with him," whispered Noelle, her voice low near his ear.

Taking deep breaths, Beanie glanced left, through the driver's window.

The man who'd walked in front of the SUV was on the ground.

"Oh my God, babe, did I hit him?" Shaking, Beanie popped the buckle on his seat belt and pushed the harness away.

"I don't think so," said Noelle. "Oh God, I hope not …"

Beanie opened the door, jumped out of the SUV, and hurried to the man. Kneeling next to him, Beanie asked, "Are you okay? Can you hear me?"

Faint dock lights from the marina shone across the road, casting a muted orange glow over the man. Through the dim gloom, Beanie could make out a dark, wet stain on the man's back. Was it … blood? A shudder passed through Beanie. Had he hit the man? He didn't think so, but maybe—

"Is he hurt?"

Startled, Beanie glanced up over his shoulder. Her expression pinched with concern, Noelle stood behind him, focused on the man lying in the middle of the road.

"I think so," answered Beanie. "We need to call the police. And an ambulance."

Nodding, Noelle ran back to the SUV.

"Listen, we're gonna get you some help, okay?" said Beanie, wondering if the man was conscious. "Can you hear me?"

A low groan told Beanie the guy was still alive.

Relieved, Beanie said, "You're gonna be okay. My wife is calling—"

The groan grew louder, turning into a wailing moan as the man's body jerked.

"Try to stay calm, please," said Beanie, trying to remember details from the CPR class he'd taken years ago. Was he still even certified?

"… shot me …" the man gasped, the words sputtering from his mouth. "… shot me …"

"What?" Beanie didn't understand. "What did you say? What—"

Crying out, the man pushed himself up and flipped over onto his back.

Losing his balance, Beanie fell back onto his hip, but then quickly righted himself and crawled to the man.

" … shot … me …" the man wheezed.

Beanie stared at him.

His heart dropped into his stomach.

The man's face, bathed in the dim light from the marina, was familiar.

A face he recognized.

His mind racing, feeling as though he'd been punched in the gut, Beanie stared into the eyes of Dr. Henry Montague.

"Shot … me …"

"Henry, what happened?" asked Beanie. "Who shot you?"

" … Robyn …" whispered Henry.

Beanie's stomach twisted. "What did you say?"

"Shot me …" Henry's eyes widened as his body trembled. "Robyn … shot me …"

7

Robyn ... shot me ...

Dr. Henry Montague's words floated through Beanie's mind, confusing and rattling him.

Beanie didn't understand. Why would Henry have said Robyn shot him? That wasn't true. Couldn't be. Henry must have been disoriented. Must have been hallucinating. The man had been shot. Losing a lot of blood. Obviously, out of his mind.

Robyn ... shot me ...

Beanie didn't believe it. Couldn't believe it. Wouldn't believe it.

Despite the balmy midnight air, Beanie shivered.

Several yards away from where they stood, in front of the SUV, cops and crime scene techs milled about the area. Three police cars, lights flashing blue and red, formed a wide berth around Henry's body. A few cops huddled together while paramedics loitered around the back of an ambulance, talking, most likely waiting for the M.E. to arrive so the death of Dr. Henry Montague could be declared, and they could put the body on a stretcher and transport it to the morgue.

"Babe ... " whispered Noelle. "I think the police want to talk to us."

Beanie glanced at Noelle. His wife's expression was wary as she looked toward the man walking over to them. Dressed in a light-colored lightweight suit, he was a young, clean-cut islander with a stern, tense expression. Beanie recognized the guy as Detective Allen Green. New to the St. Killian police force, Det. Green had transferred from the St. Felipe department several months ago.

Beanie took a deep breath. His heart thudded in anticipation of the detective's inquiry. Beanie had been introduced to Det. Green while investigating a story a few weeks ago. He remembered the young lawman as sincere and earnest, with a sympathetic nature. He was different from Detective Philippi Janvier, who jumped to conclusions and based his theories on confirmation bias.

Beanie took a step back, giving himself a moment to get his thoughts together. He hated the sly panic snaking through him, but he had good reason to be jittery considering that he was going to lie to the detective. He didn't want to, but he had to. For now, anyway. Beanie took a quick breath. He had to be convincing. He couldn't stammer or stutter. Couldn't give the detective reason to doubt him. Couldn't let Det. Green trick him into saying something he needed to stay quiet about.

Robyn ... shot me.

After quick, terse greetings, Detective Green said, "I understand that the two of you spoke to the responding officers. But I'd like you to tell me what happened if you don't mind."

Glancing at Noelle, Beanie shook his head. "Of course, we don't mind."

"We want to help you find out who killed Henry," said Noelle.

"And how do you know Dr. Henry Montague?" asked Det. Green as he swiped a finger across the display of his phone.

"He was my sister-in-law's boyfriend," said Noelle.

"Your sister-in-law?" asked Det. Green, still looking at his phone.

"My sister," said Beanie, feeling his heartbeat increasing. "Robyn Bean."

Det. Green said, "Officer Rambla said you were driving along Marina Killian Way when you saw the victim lying in the street."

"That's right," said Beanie, his mind flooded with images of the gruesome discovery.

"And what time was that?" asked Green.

Beanie tried to think. "Maybe about thirty minutes ago."

"So, around …" The detective glanced at his wrist, then frowned. "You have the time. I forgot my watch."

Glancing at his phone, Beanie recited the time, then said, "So, yeah, I was driving along Marina Killian Way and then—"

"No, that's not right," said Noelle.

Confused, his heart pounding, Beanie glanced at his wife.

"We were driving, and we saw a man *walking* into the middle of the road," said Noelle. "And then I screamed at Roland to watch out, and—"

"Right, right," said Beanie, clearing his throat. "I'm sorry. I'm still a bit shell-shocked."

"Yeah, I understand," said Det. Green.

"My wife is right," said Beanie, worried the detective might be developing doubts about his version of the events in question. "I was driving. Henry stumbled into the street and—"

"But you didn't know it was Dr. Montague?"

Beanie shook his head. "No, I didn't."

"When did you realize that the man was Dr. Montague?"

"I swerved the car so I wouldn't hit him," said Beanie.

"And then Henry collapsed in the street," said Noelle. "Roland got out and I called the police."

"I ran to help him," said Beanie. "I didn't know he'd been shot. I didn't know what had happened to him. Didn't know if he'd had a heart attack or was drunk. He was moaning. I told him to stay calm because my wife was calling an ambulance. Then he flipped himself over onto his back and that's when I saw it was Henry."

"When you approached him, he was still alive," said Det. Green, using his thumbs to type notes into his phone.

Nodding, Beanie said, "Yeah, but barely."

"He say anything to you?"

"Did he say anything?" parroted Beanie, his voice an octave too high as his heart slammed. He didn't want to lie to Det. Green, but he didn't want to tell the detective Henry had whispered that Robyn had shot him. "No, I don't think so …"

Det. Green stared at him. "Did you ask him what happened to him?"

"I think I did," said Beanie.

"And what did he tell you?"

Beanie cleared his throat. "He was moaning a lot. He might have been trying to say something, but … I don't know."

Noelle said, "I can't believe Henry is dead. I just saw him."

"Where?" Det. Green asked.

"At Roland and Robyn's thirtieth birthday party," Noelle said.

"Big three-oh, huh?" asked Det. Green.

Nodding, Beanie focused on maintaining eye contact with the detective, not avoiding his gaze.

"I'm going to hit that milestone myself in two years," said Det. Green. "I know it's coming but I'm still not quite ready for it."

"Yeah," said Beanie, wary of the amicable small talk. Not knowing much about Det. Green, Beanie wasn't sure if the man was partial to the "good cop" routine. Was the detective trying to get him to let his guard down? Did Det. Green hope Beanie would slip up and reveal something he wanted to keep hidden? If so, that meant the detective suspected Beanie was keeping something from him, but why would he? Had Beanie already telegraphed an unconscious "tell?" Despite his best efforts, Beanie might have given Det. Green a reason to suspect him. But suspect him of what? Beanie let out a slow breath. He needed to calm down and think rationally.

"So how was the party?" asked Det. Green.

"It was fun," said Noelle. "Everyone had a good time."

"And what about Dr. Montague?" asked Det. Green. "He have a good time?"

"As far as we know," said Beanie.

Det. Green gave him a sharp look. "As far as you know?"

"I mean, yeah, he had a good time," said Beanie, mentally kicking himself. "He seemed to be having a good time, but I wasn't watching him, or anything."

"The party was for Roland and his sister," said Noelle. "So, he and Robyn were the center of attention."

Det. Green nodded. "But, when you did happen to see Dr. Montague, he was having a good time?"

Beanie said, "Yeah."

"So he was mingling? Dancing?"

Beanie said, "Henry was having a good time."

"Except …" Noelle trailed off.

Glancing at Noelle, Beanie worried what his wife would say.

"Except?" prompted Det. Green.

"There was this woman who came to the party," said Noelle. "Henry's ex-girlfriend."

"And her name?" requested Detective Green.

"Dr. Liz Adams," Beanie said.

Noelle said, "She made a scene and Henry escorted her out."

"What kind of scene?" asked Det. Green.

"I think she was drunk," said Beanie. "Can't remember what she said word for word."

"What was the gist of it?" Det. Green asked.

"She was upset because Henry broke up with her," Noelle said. "She crashed the party."

"Did Dr. Adams and Dr. Montague break up recently?" asked Green. "Or was it some time ago?"

"I'm not sure," said Noelle.

Beanie said, "I'm sure Robyn would know."

"Speaking of Robyn," started Det. Green.

Beanie's pulse jumped.

"I'll send an officer over to her place to bring her to the police station," said the detective. "Maybe the two of you want to head to the station, as well. We can get formal statements on the record."

"That's fine," said Beanie, anxious for an opportunity to speak with his sister before Det. Green interrogated her.

"The M.E. just arrived and I'm going to have a few words with her," said Det. Green. "I'll meet you at the station in half an hour, or so."

8

Glancing around the witness waiting room at the St. Killian police department, Beanie took a deep breath.

The spacious room, with its comfortable chairs and pale blue walls, was designed to put people at ease, but Beanie felt his pulse ratcheting up. Since Noelle's arrest two years ago, Beanie tried his best to avoid the St. Killian police station. He couldn't help remembering the last time he'd been in the witness room. He and Noelle had come to the station to meet with Detective Philippi Janvier. Beanie had thought they were going to get a status update on Noelle's stolen car. Instead, Noelle had been arrested after Janvier accused her of murder.

Beanie pinched the bridge of his nose. He wasn't suspicious by nature, but he couldn't shake the horrible feeling of déjà vu snaking through him. He hated thinking that, once again, someone he loved was going to be arrested. He hated thinking that Robyn was going to be arrested, because ... why would she?

Robyn ... shot me ...

With a quick exhale, Beanie cautioned himself to think logically. Just because Henry had said Robyn shot him didn't mean it was true. There was no proof that Robyn had shot Henry. There was no evidence against his sister. But what did that matter? There hadn't been any evidence against Noelle but that hadn't stopped Detective Janvier from arresting her.

"I just got off the phone with Tricia," said Noelle, sitting next to him. "The boys are okay. They're sleeping."

Beanie nodded. "Good."

Dropping her phone into her purse, Noelle asked, "You okay, babe?"

Glancing at his wife, Beanie tried to give her a reassuring smile. "Just tired. Didn't think we'd be sitting in the police station at midnight."

"I hear you," said Noelle, reaching for his hand.

Lacing his fingers between his wife's, Beanie said, "We shouldn't have consented to give our formal statements right now. We already talked to the deputy and Det. Green. They know what happened."

"We might as well get it over and done with," said Noelle.

Beanie rubbed the back of his neck. "I don't see what the problem would have been with us giving our statements later, maybe after we'd gotten some sleep."

"I think we should do it while it's still fresh in our minds."

Saying nothing, Beanie sighed. He didn't want to think about what was fresh in his mind. He didn't want any more thoughts about Henry lying on the ground, gasping his last breaths.

Robyn ... shot me ...

"Mr. and Mrs. Bean?"

Glancing up, Beanie focused on the police officer standing in front of them.

"Detective Janvier wants to see you now," said the officer. "Please come with me."

Beanie's stomach lurched. "Detective Janvier wants to see us?"

"Why?" asked Noelle.

"We were supposed to meet with Det. Green," said Beanie, jaw clenched as he took his wife's hand and squeezed it, hoping to reassure her. "He's supposed to take our statements."

The officer said, "Det. Green got sent on another call. Det. Janvier is waiting. This way, please ..."

Fighting disappointment and frustration, Beanie stood, and helped Noelle to her feet. As they followed the officer down a pale-yellow hallway illuminated by harsh fluorescent overhead lights, Beanie felt as though he was being marched to the guillotine.

Beanie had thanked his lucky stars when Det. Green had shown up at the crime scene. He'd been dreading another contentious confrontation with Detective Philippi Janvier, the man who'd almost ruined his life. Several years ago, Noelle had been accused of a heinous murder. A vicious crime she hadn't committed. Janvier had been assigned to the case. The bumbling detective declared her guilty and set about to prove his suspicions, despite the lack of evidence. Even when it became clear that his wife had been framed, Janvier maintained his misguided belief. Lives had been lost due to his incompetence, but he'd never suffered any censure or formal rebuke.

Moments later, in Janvier's office, Beanie and Noelle sat side by side in the chairs in front of the detective's desk. Beanie held Noelle's hand, squeezing her fingers in a show of support and solidarity. They'd faced Janvier before. Once, he'd been a giant obstacle, but they'd overcome him. And they would again if the detective tried to take them down.

"Mr. and Mrs. Bean," snipped Janvier, leaning back in his chair. "We meet again. And, once again, we are forced to endure each other because of murder."

Glaring at the detective, Beanie wasn't surprised by the scorn in the man's narrowed gaze or the derision in Janvier's haughty tone. He also wasn't surprised Janvier hadn't missed the opportunity to bring up the traumatic events he and Noelle wanted to forget.

"A man is dead," Janvier snapped, dark eyes flashing. "Struck down like a dog by a killer. Shot to death. Which is horrible. But, not as heinous as beating a man to death with a shovel, no?"

Noelle's quick intake of breath made Beanie's chest tighten. He wanted to slug the detective and might have done it, but he suspected Janvier wanted him to lash out. The detective was itching to put someone with the last name Bean in jail. Janvier was still upset that he'd been wrong about Noelle. He'd looked like an incompetent fool when the real murderer was revealed.

"Well, I actually wouldn't know," said Noelle. "I've never beaten a man to death with a shovel."

A vein bulged near Janvier's temple.

"As you know," added Beanie. "As you should have known or would have known if you hadn't ignored the evidence."

Janvier blanched for a second before his face went crimson. Yanking a file from an Inbox tray and a pen from a round, wire mesh pencil holder, he asked, "How do you know the victim?"

With Noelle's input, Beanie explained his relationship with Dr. Henry Montague.

Janvier's eyes narrowed as he glared at them. "The victim is your sister's boyfriend, you say. And your sister's name?"

"Robyn Bean."

"And how long had your sister and the victim been involved?"

"About three months," said Noelle, and Beanie nodded his agreement.

"A relatively new relationship," remarked Janvier, scribbling on a document in the file. "How were things going?"

"What do you mean?" asked Beanie, trying to ignore the sly apprehension seeping into him.

Janvier glanced up. "How would you describe the relationship between your sister and the victim?"

Clearing his throat, Beanie took a glance at Noelle, then said, "I'm not sure how I would describe it. Maybe I don't understand your question."

Leaning back in his chair, Janvier smiled. "You must have observed interactions between your sister and the victim, no?"

Annoyed by the detective's Cheshire grin, Beanie said, "On occasion, yes."

"On what occasions?" asked Janvier.

"We've had dinner with Robyn and Henry," said Noelle. "Gone to the movies together a few times. Done things that couples do together."

"Were Robyn and Henry in love?"

"As far as I could tell," said Noelle.

Beanie nodded, though he didn't necessarily agree. He'd observed a definite tension between his sister and Henry, which had culminated in their argument at the birthday party.

"Did you ever observe any issues between the two?" asked Janvier.

The apprehension in Beanie's gut grew. "Issues?"

"Problems? Fights?" clarified Janvier. "Arguments?"

Beanie struggled to read the detective's shrewd, piercing stare. Was Janvier fishing for something? Trying to catch Beanie in a lie? But why would the detective be suspicious of him? Maybe because Janvier was suspicious by nature? Or maybe because Beanie *was* hiding something, and Janvier could tell he wasn't being completely honest with him.

Pushing the memory of Robyn's argument with Henry from his mind, Beanie said, "I don't recall."

Peripherally, Beanie saw Noelle glance at him.

"What about you Mrs. Bean," said Janvier. "Ever seen your sister-in-law and her beau at odds?"

Shaking her head, Noelle said, "No …"

Following more scribbling in the file, Janvier said, "Tell me a bit more about the thirtieth birthday party." "What about the party?" asked Noelle.

Janvier asked, "Who did Henry talk to at the party?"

Beanie answered, "Lots of people."

"I'd like to have the names of everyone you remember Dr. Montague talking to at the party," said Janvier.

Noelle said, "Mostly, I saw him talking to Robyn and their friends from the hospital."

"What friends from the hospital?" asked Janvier.

Beanie cleared his throat. "Dr. Emily Taylor and her fiancée, Tim. Another nurse named Sara."

"I can email you the guest list," said Noelle.

Janvier asked, "Was Dr. Montague having a good time at the party?"

Beanie stared at the detective. "What do you mean?"

The detective stared back at him. "Was Dr. Montague laughing and joking with his friends?"

Noelle nodded. "Yes. He was having a good time."

"All night?" asked Janvier.

"As far as I saw," said Noelle. "Well, he was up until his ex-girlfriend showed up uninvited."

Janvier leaned back in his chair. "Tell me more about that."

Noelle let out a breath, and then detailed the moment when the ex had crashed the party.

Janvier asked, "So the only time Dr. Montague wasn't having a good time was when his ex-girlfriend showed up?"

"Yeah," said Beanie. "I guess."

"And what about Robyn and Dr. Montague?" asked Janvier. "They were having a good time?"

Noelle nodded. "Great time."

"Until the ex-girlfriend showed up," said Janvier.

"Right," said Beanie, his pulse racing. "But after she left, everything was fine again."

Scribbling on the papers in the file, Janvier said, "Tell me why you were out on the road so late at night."

Noelle said, "We were going to check on Robyn. She'd called Roland because someone had broken into her home."

Beanie said, "I told her to call the police and that Noelle, and I would head over there."

Janvier nodded. "Interesting."

"What?" asked Beanie.

Janvier said, "There's no report of a call from your sister about a break-in at her place."

Beanie was confused, shocked. "Are you sure?"

The detective frowned.

Beanie said, "I told Robyn to call the cops."

Janvier said, "Well, she didn't."

Shaking his head, Beanie said, "I don't know why she wouldn't have …"

"Mr. Bean, do you know of anyone who would want to shoot the victim?" asked Janvier. "Or do you know why someone might want to shoot him?"

Beanie recalled the gun Henry had obtained to protect himself against his unstable ex-girlfriend, Dr. Liz Adams. Could Dr. Adams have shot Henry? Where had the woman gone after Henry escorted her out of the party? Maybe she'd headed to Henry's townhouse to hide, laying in wait until Henry returned. She might have seen Henry leave the townhouse for his nocturnal run. She could have followed him. Shot him. She'd pulled a gun on him before. Maybe tonight, Dr. Liz Adams had made good on the threat to kill Henry.

Beanie supposed he could bring up the fact that Dr. Adams had stalked Henry, and tried to kill him, but it was uncorroborated secondhand information. And if it wasn't true, if Henry had embellished the tale, Janvier would certainly accuse Beanie of blatantly lying to impede the investigation. Which Beanie would never do. He had no reason to. He might have a reason to obstruct justice if he was trying to protect someone. Like his sister. *Robyn ... shot me.* Only his sister hadn't shot Henry, so she didn't need protecting. So, maybe he should—

"Mr. Bean ..." prompted Janvier.

Deciding to keep details about Henry's psycho former lover to himself, for now, Beanie shook his head.

"No, I don't," he said, aware of Noelle glancing at him. Did his wife think he should have mentioned Henry's crazy ex-girlfriend? Did Noelle think he was staying quiet to protect Robyn? But why would Noelle think he needed to protect Robyn? Noelle didn't know about Henry's dying, gasping last words.

Robyn ... shot me.

Janvier made an odd sound as he pulled his bottom lip. "Perhaps your sister might know."

"I'm not sure if she would, or not," said Beanie.

"Well, let's let her tell us," said Janvier, picking up the receiver from the phone on his desk. "Bring Ms. Bean to my office."

"I'd like to speak with my sister before you talk to her," requested Beanie, hoping to confer with his sister before Janvier grilled her. He worried about Robyn talking to Janvier. Worried about what she might say. Worried about what she might not say.

"And why should I let you do that?" sneered Janvier. "So you can warn your sister? Help her come up with some cockamamie story so she won't look guilty."

"Why would I need to warn my sister?" asked Beanie, worried Janvier had already decided that Robyn was guilty.

"Your impertinent request is denied," said Janvier. "I will not allow you to conspire and collude with your sister."

Seconds later, Robyn entered. She looked worried and annoyed as her eyes darted back and forth, from Beanie and Noelle to Det. Janvier. Beanie recognized his sister's expression. Her glare communicated a reluctance to be bothered, but she was resigned to deal with the present situation.

Standing, Beanie walked toward Robyn as she hurried to him. "Is it true?" she asked. "Is Henry really dead?" After a quick, reassuring hug, Beanie nodded. "I'm sorry …"

"Oh my God," whispered Robyn. "How? What happened? The officer wouldn't tell me anything."

Janvier said, "Have a seat, Ms. Bean."

"Why don't you tell me what happened to Henry," demanded Robyn, arms crossed.

"We'll get to that," said Janvier.

With a sigh of irritation, Robyn sat in the chair Beanie had vacated. "Okay …"

"Mr. Bean, I have no more questions for you and your wife. At this time," said Janvier. "The two of you can leave now."

Beanie said, "I'd like to stay."

"That won't be necessary," said Janvier. "I need to question Ms. Bean alone."

Shaking his head, Beanie said, "I don't think that's a good—"

"I'll be okay, Roland," said Robyn, her gaze confident as she gave him a stare he recognized. A look to remind him that she was not only his big sister but a grown woman who could handle her business.

"I don't mind staying," said Beanie.

"It'll be fine," said Robyn, her tone firm. "Don't worry."

Noelle stood and placed a comforting hand on Beanie's forearm. "Let's go back to the waiting room, okay?"

Beanie didn't like being dismissed but figured there wasn't anything he could do about it, considering that Robyn was consenting to the police interview.

9

In the waiting room, Noelle said, "I know you're going to worry about Robyn, but I don't think you should. Your sister can handle herself."

"How can you say that?" asked Beanie, pacing in front of the couch where Noelle sat. "Janvier jumps to the wrong conclusion without any supporting evidence. And he probably subscribes to the theory that the person closest to the victim is the most likely suspect. You know when the husband is killed, the wife did it, and vice versa."

"So, what if Janvier starts jumping to conclusions?" asked Noelle.

Beanie stopped pacing to gape at his wife. "Are you serious?"

"It'll be the wrong conclusion," said Noelle. "Robyn hasn't done anything wrong."

Henry's last words filled Beanie's mind. *Robyn ... shot me.*

"Babe ..." prompted Noelle.

Shaking away the disturbing thoughts, Beanie said, "I just don't want Robyn to say something that might get her into trouble."

Noelle frowned. "What could she say that would get her in trouble?"

Beanie dragged a hand down his face. "I don't know, I just ..."

"Come sit down, Roland," said Noelle, patting the cushion next to her.

Sinking down next to his wife, Beanie put his arm around her and kissed her cheek. "You're right. I shouldn't worry, but you know my sister can be a know-it-all."

"A sarcastic know-it-all," corrected Noelle.

Beanie chuckled. "Exactly. And that attitude of hers might upset Janvier. And then he might trick her into saying something that makes her look suspicious."

"Are you worried that Janvier might think Robyn killed Henry?" asked Noelle. "Because that's ridiculous."

Robyn ... shot me. Beanie couldn't get Henry's words out of his head. They weren't true, he knew. They couldn't be, and yet they scared him. Those words were could cause a lot of trouble for Robyn, trouble Beanie wanted to spare his sister, which was why he was keeping those words to himself. For now, anyway. He didn't want to repeat those whispered words, gasped from the mouth of a dying man who'd been disoriented and confused. At least not until he spoke with Robyn first.

"I'm worried about this whole situation," said Beanie. "I'm worried for Robyn. And I'm worried that a murderer is out there on the loose. Someone who shot a man in cold blood and left him to die in the street."

"I'm so glad you guys are still here," said Robyn, walking into the waiting room.

"What did Janvier ask you?" Beanie jumped up. "What did you tell him?"

Shaking her head, Robyn sighed. "Can we please talk about it tomorrow?"

Beanie asked, "He didn't try to trick you into incriminating yourself, did he?"

Robyn pinched the bridge of her nose. "Tomorrow, little brother, okay? I'll tell you everything. Word for word."

Frustrated, Beanie said, "But, just tell me—"

"I told you we will talk about this tomorrow," snapped Robyn. "Right now, I just want to go home so can you please drive me back to my place?"

Beanie balked. "You want to go back to the townhouse?"

Noelle said, "Why don't you come home with us?"

"Thank you for the offer," said Robyn. "I appreciate it, but—"

"You can't go back," Beanie told his sister.

Robyn frowned. "Why not?"

"Someone killed Henry," said Beanie. "Shot him to death. What if that person shows up at the townhouse? What if they want to hurt you, too?"

"Roland, don't let your over-active investigative imagination run wild," cautioned Robyn. "I'll be okay at the townhouse."

Noelle said, "But, someone broke in—"

"No one broke into the house," said Robyn, exhaling.

Confused, Beanie frowned. "What?"

Robyn exhaled. "I was mistaken."

Beanie stared at his twin. "Mistaken?"

Shrugging, Robyn said, "I told you I wasn't sure if someone had broken in, or not. Turns out, I was wrong."

"Why didn't you call the police like I told you to?" asked Beanie.

"Because I didn't need the police," said Robyn, crossing her arms. "Listen, if you don't want to give me a ride, fine. I'll take a cab, or—"

"You don't have to take a cab," said Beanie. "We'll take you home."

"Listen, I just … " Robyn shook her head. "I'm just shocked and confused about what happened to Henry and I need to be alone right now. This is hard for me to wrap my head around."

"We understand," said Noelle.

Beanie put an arm around his sister. "You sure you're going to be okay?"

Glancing up at him, Robyn nodded, giving him a small, sad smile.

Grabbing Noelle's hand, Beanie said, "Okay, then let's get out of here."

10

Staggering into the kitchen, Beanie blinked his bleary eyes against the harsh, bright rays of sun glaring through the window above the sink.

"Well, if it isn't Rip Van Winkle," sang out Noelle, walking toward him with a cup of coffee.

Chuckling, Beanie stumbled over to the table, pulled out a chair, and dropped down into it. "Babe, I think I slept more than forty winks. Feels like I fell into a coma."

"This should help you out of it," said Noelle, placing the coffee mug in front of him.

"What time is it?" asked Beanie, taking a sip of coffee.

"Noon," said Noelle.

Beanie took a few more sips of the strong, fortifying brew. "We had quite a long night."

"Too long," Noelle laughed as she sat across from him.

Rubbing his eyes, Beanie exhaled. "What time did we finally get to bed?"

"After we took Robyn home," said Noelle, "I texted Tricia—"

"To tell her we'd pick up the boys in the morning," said Beanie, remembering. "But she was up so she told us it was okay to stop by and get them."

"I think it was close to two in the morning by then," said Noelle.

"Did the alarm go off?" asked Beanie, lifting the coffee mug to his lips again.

"I think it did, but I didn't hear it," said Noelle. "We missed church."

"The boys are up?"

Noelle took a sip of coffee. "Playing in the backyard. I'm going to go out there and catch up on some reading. After a second cup of coffee."

"I would join you, but ..."

"But?"

Thinking of his sister, and Henry's murder, and Det. Janvier's sly interrogation, Beanie said, "I need to call Robyn. I need to find out what Janvier asked her. Find out what she told him. I need to know what happened last night."

"I can't believe Henry is dead," said Noelle.

Nodding, Beanie said, "Makes you think about how one day you can be here, and the next day ... you're gone."

Noelle winced. "I don't like to think about that. But, still, I wonder who killed him. You think maybe he was robbed?"

Robyn ... shot me ...

Pushing away the worrisome memory, Beanie said, "I haven't had much time to think about it, but ... now that we're discussing it, I can't help thinking about the psycho ex-girlfriend. She showed up at the party unannounced. Maybe she showed up at the townhouse to continue her tirade against Henry."

"But Henry was staggering down the road near the marina," reminded Noelle.

Standing, Noelle picked up her coffee mug and took it to the kitchen sink. "Okay, then, if Dr. Adams confronted Henry and shot him at the townhouse, why was he near the marina?"

"Maybe Dr. Adams didn't shoot him at the townhouse," suggested Beanie. "Maybe she convinced him to meet her somewhere. Maybe at the marina, which is not far from the townhouse. It's actually behind the complex. About a five-minute walk away. Dr. Adams might have shot him, and Henry tried to get away. He staggered into the street and I almost hit him."

Leaning against the counter, arms crossed, Noelle nodded. "That's possible. Could have been a crime of passion. If she couldn't have Henry, then no one could have Henry."

Beanie stroked his jaw, pondering his wife's theory. He liked the idea of a crazy ex killing the good doctor better than the idea of his sister getting rid of her boyfriend. *Robyn ... shot me.* Despite Henry's dying words, Beanie couldn't believe them. But why had Henry said those words? If Dr. Adams had shot him, why hadn't Henry fingered the psycho ex-girlfriend as his killer?

"Why didn't you tell Janvier about the psycho ex-girlfriend when he asked you who might have killed Henry?" asked Noelle. "I mean, I get why you didn't mention the argument Robyn and Henry had in the boys' bedroom—"

"Because I didn't want to give Janvier a reason to jump to the wrong conclusion."

Noelle nodded. "Exactly. That's why I didn't mention it, either. But you could have given Janvier a suspect to check out. I wanted to tell him about Liz Adams, but when you didn't say anything, I figured you'd stayed quiet for a reason."

Beanie glanced at his wife. "I didn't mention the ex because I didn't think Janvier would take me seriously."

Shrugging, Noelle asked, "You're probably right, but ..."

"But what?"

"It's just so weird that Henry was killed and then Robyn thought someone broke into her home."

Bothered by the slight suspicion in his wife's gaze, Beanie asked, "What do you mean?"

Noelle asked, "What if someone did break into the townhouse?"

"But, no one did," said Beanie. "Robyn was mistaken."

"Unless she wasn't mistaken," said Noelle. "Maybe— "

"Daddy! Mommy!"

Beanie jumped as his boys came running into the kitchen. Ethan skipped as he whooped and yelled, while little Evan tried his best to keep up with his brother, squealing and clapping, running as fast as his chubby little legs could carry him.

Beanie hurried to the boys, meeting them halfway. He scooped up Ethan and Evan and turned around in a circle as they held on to him. Their delighted screams made Beanie's heart soar and filled him with a joy that was indescribable and hard to explain.

"Can we go to Loco Goat, Daddy?" asked Ethan. Loco Goat, a family-friendly dining establishment popular with tourists and residents, was the boys' favorite restaurant.

"Sure, we can go to Loco Goat," said Beanie, kissing the boys' foreheads as he sank to one knee on the ceramic tile, lowering the boys to the floor.

Behind him, Noelle cleared her throat.

Beanie glanced up at his wife. "If Mommy thinks it's okay ..."

Ethan ran to Noelle. "Mommy, can we go to Loco Goat? Please! Please! Please!"

"Please, Mommy!" repeated Evan, hugging one of Noelle's legs as he stared up at her. "Loco Goat! Please!"

"Okay, we can go to Loco Goat," agreed Noelle, crouching to kiss the boys before they ran out of the kitchen, singing loud and off-key about the trip to Loco Goat.

Noelle walked over to Beanie. "A trip to Loco Goat? You think that was necessary?"

Sheepish, Beanie shrugged. "I feel bad because the birthday party was adults only and the boys were initially upset that they had to stay with Tricia."

Noelle asked, "You think Robyn might want to join us? Maybe an outing with her rowdy nephews might take her mind off what happened to Henry for a few hours."

Beanie shook his head. "I don't think so. But I do plan to go over to the townhouse and check on her after we leave the restaurant. I need to find out about her conversation with Janvier. I hate that he's been assigned to Henry's murder."

"I don't think you have anything to worry about," said Noelle.

"Elle, we're talking about Detective Janvier," said Beanie. "He falsely accused you of murder and tried to put you in jail for the rest of your life. I don't want the same thing to happen to my sister."

"Janvier is not going to accuse Robyn of murder," said Noelle. "That's ridiculous. There's no way that Robyn shot Henry."

"You're right," said Beanie, though he wasn't exactly sure. "My sister is not a killer."

11

"How are you holding up?" Beanie asked Robyn, stepping through the double doors and into the spacious foyer of the three-story townhouse his sister had shared with Dr. Henry Montague.

Located in Adagio Bay, a community of luxury developments surrounding the marina, the townhouse featured traditional Caribbean Colonial architecture and was decorated in a style that Beanie would call "tropical glamour." The soothing neutral color scheme mimicked shades of the beach: pale aqua, sand, and foamy white. Within the large rooms were high-end rattan and mahogany furniture, and large indoor palm trees in huge decorative pots. Natural fiber rugs covered the bamboo flooring. Ceiling to floor glass walls offered stunning views of the Caribbean and the tall Queen palm trees surrounding the property.

"I'm okay, I guess." Sighing, Robyn closed the door and led the way into the spacious living area, an open concept design where the family room flowed into the kitchen which flowed into a large dining area.

"You guess?" questioned Beanie, concerned as he followed his sister into the dining room.

Robyn blew out a breath as she walked to the opposite end of the long teakwood table where a large cardboard Banker's box sat on the gleaming surface.

"Tell me the truth." Beanie sat down in one of the bamboo dining chairs. "How are you doing?"

Frowning, Robyn pointed at him. "What's that on your shirt?"

"What?" Beanie glanced down. "Oh. Jerk sauce."

"Jerk sauce?"

"Noelle and I took the boys to Loco Goat," said Beanie. "Evan got a little messy."

Running a hand through her long, crinkly hair, Robyn chuckled. "Bet that was fun."

"The boys had a good time." After their impromptu trip to the popular, family-friendly restaurant, they'd taken a walk through the neighborhood park so the boys could play on the playground. As the sun began to set, they pushed the boys in the swings, down the slide, and Beanie helped the boys cross the monkey bars.

They headed home around seven. After bath time, the kiddos were tuckered out, too tired for their customary bedtime story. Beanie didn't mind so much. He loved reading to his boys, but he was anxious to talk to Robyn about Henry's murder.

While he and Noelle were at Loco Goat with the boys, Beanie ruminated on Henry's dying words.

Robyn ... shot me. Beanie would get anxious, but then Ethan would do something funny to distract him. However, the distraction wouldn't last, and the memories of Henry staggering in the road would creep back into his mind, and the investigative reporter in him would have a million questions.

Robyn ... shot me.

Beanie still wasn't sure if he wanted to tell Robyn. He didn't want to scare his sister, but he had to find out why Henry would accuse Robyn of shooting him.

"Tell me about the interview with Janvier," requested Beanie.

"Not much to tell," said Robyn, reaching into the Banker's box, and pulling out a thin manila file folder. "He just asked me what happened last night."

"And what did you tell him?"

Glancing away, Robyn opened the file.

"No, forget what you told Janvier," said Beanie. "Tell me the truth."

His sister glared at him. "What makes you think I didn't tell Janvier the truth?"

Beanie exhaled, struggling to temper his frustration. "What happened last night?"

"After the party, Henry and I went home," said Robyn, perusing documents in the file. "I was really tired, but Henry wasn't, so he told me he was going for a run on the beach."

"A run on the beach at night?" Beanie couldn't hide his doubt.

Placing the file on the table next to the box, Robyn nodded. "He does that a lot. Says it clears his head. Anyway, I went to bed."

"Henry was still out on his run?" asked Beanie.

Nodding, Robyn said, "So, I'm sleeping when I hear a noise coming from the living room. I sit up in bed. I'm groggy and I call out to Henry because I think it's him, but I just hear more noises. Immediately, I'm wide awake and trying not to panic. I grab the gun. Well, at first, I couldn't find it—"

"You couldn't find the gun?" asked Beanie. "Wait. You're talking about the gun Henry got for protection from his crazy ex, Dr. Liz Adams?"

"It was in the wrong drawer," Robyn explained. "So, I got the gun, got out of bed, and tiptoed into the living room. I heard more noises, and I thought I saw a shadow run past the glass pocket doors that lead out to the terrace. I fired the gun twice. And then I thought I saw the shadow slip out of the pocket doors, which were open—"

"Because you wanted to take advantage of the sea breeze?" asked Beanie, remembering the explanation she'd given him earlier.

"And because Henry leaves the townhouse that way when he heads to the beach," said Robyn. "So, I slipped out of the pocket doors and I took a look around the terrace but I didn't see anything. So, I went back into the townhouse. I closed the pocket doors, and called you."

Frowning, Beanie asked, "And you're sure there was no one on the terrace?"

"I told you I didn't see anyone," said Robyn, shrugging as she reached into the Banker's box and extracted more documents. "Now that I think about it, I probably saw my neighbor's cat or something. Maybe I was seeing things. As you know, I partied a little too hard."

Pinching the bridge of his nose, Beanie reflected on his sister's version of the events. Her story sounded plausible, and of course, he believed her, but he had the feeling she was keeping something from him.

Robyn said, "Speaking of the gun …"

Beanie waited, trying not to think the worst.

"I didn't tell the cops about it," said Robyn.

Worried, Beanie asked, "Why not?"

Robyn shrugged. "I didn't want to tell Janvier that I was shooting at shadows."

"Did you tell him you thought someone had broken into the townhouse?"

"No, I didn't," said Robyn, opening another manila file. "Because no one broke into the townhouse. I was mistaken, remember?"

"What did you tell Janvier?" asked Beanie.

"Everything I just told you," said Robyn. "But I left out the part about firing the gun. I told Janvier that Henry went for a run, and I went to bed. I didn't mention anything about hearing weird noises."

Beanie asked, "Did Janvier question you about a break-in at the townhouse? Because Noelle and I told him that we were headed to your place because you'd called me and said you thought someone had broken in."

Robyn shook her head. "He didn't ask me anything about a break-in, but he did ask me …"

"He asked you … what?" prompted Beanie, his heart starting to pound.

"What is this?" Robyn frowned as she removed a small document from the file and stared at it.

"What is what?" Beanie asked, trying to stay calm, fighting frustration.

"This is so weird …"

"What is weird?" demanded Beanie. "What are you looking at? What are all those files in that box? What are you doing?"

Robyn exhaled. "The hospital sent over some boxes of Henry's things from his office. Can you believe they cleaned it out so quickly? Anyway, I was going through the files to make sure there was nothing important I needed to take care of, and I opened this file and there's a check inside."

"What kind of check?"

Robyn said, "A ten-thousand-dollar check from Mimi to Henry."

"Mimi?"

"Dr. Emily Taylor," said Robyn. "You remember I introduced you to her at the party yesterday? She was there with her fiancé, Tim."

Beanie nodded.

"Looks like Henry cashed it a month before our birthday party," said Robyn, holding the check between her thumb and index finger.

Beanie frowned. "Why would Mimi give Henry a check for ten thousand dollars?"

Shrugging, Robyn said, "I don't know."

"Henry told you he'd borrowed money from the guy you saw him with," reminded Beanie. "Told you the guy was threatening him about paying back the money."

"I also told you I didn't believe that story."

"But what if it was true," suggested Beanie. "Maybe he borrowed money from Mimi to pay back the old friend who threatened him?"

Shaking her head, Robyn said, "I doubt it. Henry and Mimi didn't know each other well. She's my friend. I introduced her to Henry. They both work at St. Killian General but Mimi's a neurologist. They didn't really cross paths."

"That you know of," said Beanie.

Robyn pulled another file out of the box. "I suppose …"

Beanie said, "Let's go back to your conversation with Janvier. You were about to tell me something that he'd asked you?"

"Janvier asked me if I killed Henry," said Robyn, placing the file on the stack of files next to the box.

"And what did you say?" asked Beanie as, once again, Henry's gasping last words filtered through his mind.

Robyn scoffed as she scowled. "What do you think I said?"

"What I meant was …" Beanie paused to collect his thoughts. "Tell me this: how did Janvier pose the question? Was he blunt and direct? Or sly and cagey?"

"What does that matter?"

"It matters because Detective Janvier jumps to conclusions, especially when he's interrogating a suspect—"

"A suspect?" Robyn stared at him. "Since when am I a suspect? I didn't have anything to do with Henry's murder. I didn't shoot him, and I told Janvier that."

Beanie rubbed his jaw kicking himself for his slip. "I know you're not a suspect, okay? That's not what I meant. I was just trying to say that you have to be really careful when you're talking to Janvier. He thinks he's smart enough to figure out who the killer is without any evidence to support his conclusion. And once he decides who his main suspect is, he works overtime to prove that his assumptions are right even when they are dead wrong. Especially when they're dead wrong. The man has a terminal case of confirmation bias. Evidence to the contrary will not convince him that he's wrong."

Robyn said, "He didn't paint me into any corners if that's what you're worried about. I gave him my story—which was the truth—and I stuck to it. He tried to confuse me by asking the same questions a hundred different ways, but I didn't fall for it, so don't worry, okay?"

"Did Janvier believe that you didn't have anything to do with Henry's murder?"

"Who knows?" Robyn sighed. "Maybe."

Beanie asked, "Did he ask you if you knew who might want to kill Henry?"

Robyn nodded. "I gave him a name. Dr. Elizabeth Adams."

"You did?"

"The more I thought about it," said Robyn, "the more I started to think that Liz probably is a homicidal psycho. You see how she crashed the party. She could be capable of anything. Even murder."

Beanie said, "True, but—"

"Hopefully, Janvier will focus on Liz Adams," said Robyn. "And not on me."

"Why would he focus on you?" asked Beanie. "You didn't kill Henry."

"But Janvier suspects me. Cops always suspect the person closest to the victim. And that's me, Henry's girlfriend."

"True," agreed Beanie.

"Anyway, Janvier promised to have more questions for me."

Beanie scoffed. "Yeah, I'm not surprised."

After a pause, Robyn said, "I have a question for you."

Glancing at his sister, Beanie was struck by her intense, sorrowful gaze. "What is it?"

"Did Henry say anything before he died?"

His gut twisting, Beanie swallowed. "What?"

"Janvier told me that Henry was still alive when you found him," said Robyn. "Did he say anything?"

Robyn ... shot me.

"Roland?" prompted Robyn.

Clearing his throat, Beanie struggled to figure out what to tell his sister. The truth wasn't an option. Not right now. Not when he had no idea why Henry had accused his sister. He didn't want to shock Robyn. Or scare her. She was grieving. She didn't need the added stress of knowing Henry had thought she'd shot him. Especially since it wasn't true. His sister hadn't killed Henry. She couldn't have.

"Did Henry tell you what happened to him?" asked Robyn.

"What happened to him?" echoed Beanie, apprehension intensifying within him.

"Did he tell you who shot him?"

Beanie stared at his sister. Why did her inquiry bother him? Why did he think it was odd that she wanted to know if Henry had uttered any last words? Hadn't Detectives Green and Janvier asked him the same question? Of course, Robyn would want to know if Henry had said anything before he'd passed away. And Beanie wanted to tell her. Wanted to be honest. But, he couldn't. Not yet.

Robyn ... shot me.

"No ..." said Beanie. "Henry didn't say anything before he died."

12

At the *Palmchat Gazette*, Beanie struggled to focus on revisions to the story he'd been sent to cover that morning, but he had trouble concentrating.

He couldn't stop thinking about the story he'd written two days ago. DOCTOR GUNNED DOWN NEAR MARINA.

The story was still getting lots of traction on the newspaper's website. It was trending on the Palmchat Gazette's social media pages, and had lots of comments, from interesting opinions to scathing judgment from trolls. Beanie sighed. The story wasn't his best work, and he hadn't wanted to write it. His involvement in the circumstances, however, convinced his Managing Editor, Vivian Thomas-Bronson, that the article would benefit from Beanie's first-person account of the horrible events. Thankfully, Vivian hadn't insisted that he mention Robyn in the article, though. Beanie had been relieved.

Other than being Henry's girlfriend, Robyn had little to add to the narrative. His sister's belief that Dr. Liz Adams had killed Henry was salacious, but Beanie decided not to mention her unfounded opinion. Also omitted from the article had been Henry's last words. *Robyn ... shot me.*

Thanks to Detective Green, who was proving more forthcoming with information than Det. Janvier, Beanie had gotten more details about the crime. The forensic pathologist had removed a bullet from Henry's back, which the crime scene technicians determined had been fired from a Glock. However, Det. Green told Beanie the cops still hadn't recovered the murder weapon.

As for suspects, Detective Green said he and Janvier were still investigating.

Beanie's thoughts pivoted to his twin sister. He prayed Janvier wouldn't start to suspect her.

He'd been thinking about what Robyn told Detective Janvier, turning her words over and over in his mind. Her account of the events of that night was missing something. What, Beanie didn't know. He couldn't shake the feeling that his sister might know more about Henry's killer than she was admitting. Nine months in the same womb had given them a unique insight into each other's feelings.

Beanie wouldn't call it a psychic link, but a special discernment. Wasn't anything creepy like the ability to read each other's minds but there were things about his sister he just knew. It was hard to explain. Beanie rubbed his jaw. He knew there was something his sister wasn't telling him. Something about what happened the night Henry was murdered.

He wondered if Noelle had been right and someone had broken into the townhouse. What Robyn assumed was a shadow could have been an intruder. Possibly Liz Adams. Or maybe the old friend Henry owed money. Maybe Liz or the old friend had broken into the townhouse, looking to confront Henry, but when he wasn't there, Liz or the old friend had slipped out of the patio.

A different scenario floated into his mind.

Suppose the killer had knocked on the door, and when Robyn opened it, the person barged in, demanding to see Henry? Robyn would have told the person Henry wasn't there, but the person could have insisted on waiting for Henry to return. Afraid for her life, Robyn could have gotten Henry's gun and fired two warning shots to convince the person to leave.

When Henry turned up dead, Robyn might have suspected that the unwanted visitor had killed Henry. Maybe she decided to stay quiet about the identity of that person, fearing she might be targeted for telling the truth.

Scratching his jaw, Beanie winced as his nail scraped the skin he'd accidentally nicked while shaving that morning.

Henry's last words arrested his attention again.

How important were the gasping words of a dying man? Should they be taken to heart? *Robyn ... shot me.* Henry's accusation had been playing in his mind since the cardiologist had uttered the words. Beanie still didn't believe the accusation was true. Robyn could not have shot Henry. She wouldn't have; his sister wasn't cold-blooded like that.

Nevertheless, Beanie had suffered a constant crisis of conscience since the night Henry died.

He shouldn't have lied to Detective Green. The man had asked him point-blank if Henry had said anything before he passed away. Beanie should have come clean about Henry's dying words. But, he hadn't. Because he'd been shell-shocked. And scared. Of what, though? Afraid maybe Henry had been telling the truth. No, that wasn't possible. So why hadn't he just told Det. Green the truth?

He'd been trying to protect Robyn. Not because his sister was guilty. She was innocent, but Henry's accusation made his sister look guilty. Det. Green would have relayed the information to Det. Janvier, the lead detective on the case, and Janvier would have arrested Robyn. Beanie couldn't let his sister go down for something she hadn't done. Something she wouldn't have done.

Beanie's phone beeped, signaling a text.

Grabbing his phone, Beanie read the message. *Hey I'm n the lobby. u have a minute 2 talk?*

Exhaling, Beanie read the text again, trying not to worry. Robyn had sent the message. Beanie rubbed his jaw. Since moving back to St. Killian, Robyn had never come to his job, not even to take him to lunch. She wasn't the type to just stop by unannounced for a quick chat. He hoped something wasn't wrong. Hoped nothing bad had happened.

Resolved not to panic, Beanie sent a reply: *sure. Give me a second.*

Five minutes later, he was sitting next to Robyn on one of the rattan sofas, on the right side of the spacious, airy lobby. Though they were far enough away from Millie, the dutiful receptionist who'd given him a quizzical look, Beanie still whispered when he asked, "What's going on?"

"I got a call from a friend at the hospital who works in IT," said Robyn.

"About what?" asked Beanie, his pounding heart slowing to a normal pace, though he didn't like the worry etched across his sister's face.

"He wants to talk to me about Henry's murder," said Robyn. "He wants me to meet him at the hospital cafeteria in thirty minutes. I'm kind of nervous about what he's going to tell me. You think you could come with me?"

"Of course," said Beanie, standing. "Let me get my phone and keys and I'll drive us over there."

Half an hour later, in the cold, austere, but well-lit cafeteria at St. Killian General Hospital, Beanie sat at a small, square table with Robyn and her friend, an IT tech named Robert. A huge, mountain of a man, Robert had a shy, gentle demeanor that seemed incongruous with his gruff exterior.

"Probably should have told the cops about this, but ..." said Robert, after quick greetings and introductions.

"But ... ?" prompted Robyn.

"What should you have told the cops?" asked Beanie.

"Don't want to get anyone in trouble," said Robert, his gaze furtive. "Maybe this isn't a good idea. Maybe I'm wasting your time. I should go—"

"No, wait ..." Robyn reached out and placed a hand on Robert's hairy forearm. "Don't leave."

Beanie said, "If you know something about Henry's murder, then you should tell us."

"I don't want to get anyone in trouble," repeated Robert, his expression distressed.

"Why do you think you'd get someone in trouble?" asked Robyn. "Who might get in trouble?"

Robert sighed, and leaned forward. Eyes darting, voice lowered, he said, "A few days ago, I was offered money to erase some emails from the hospital's backup servers."

"Erase emails?" echoed Robyn.

Nodding, Robert said, "They wanted me to make the emails go away. Make them disappear so there would be no digital traces of the emails."

"What did the emails say?" asked Robyn.

"Who wanted you to make the emails disappear?" asked Beanie.

After a moment's hesitation, his voice even lower, Robert said, "Dr. Emily Taylor …"

"Mimi?" said Robyn, frowning.

Beanie glanced from his sister to the reticent IT tech. "Why would Dr. Taylor ask you to do that?"

"If you read the emails, you'll figure it out," said Robert, reaching into the pocket of his windbreaker.

Beanie glanced at Robyn again, but his sister seemed even more confused than he was.

The IT tech pushed a folded envelope across the table. "Emails are in there. Take a look. Give them to the cops if you think they need to see them."

"These emails have something to do with Henry's murder?" asked Beanie.

"Maybe. I don't know. They seem suspicious to me, but …" Robert stood. "Read them and see what you think. I'm not trying to get anyone in trouble. Just thought you should know about them. I have to go."

As the big man lumbered away, Beanie glanced at his twin. "Well, that was …"

"Odd," said Robyn, opening the envelope.

"I was thinking weird," admitted Beanie. "But same difference."

"Oh my God …"

"What?"

Staring at the printed emails, Robyn said, "Maybe the cops do need to see these emails."

"What do they say?"

Robyn handed the printed copy to Beanie.

After reading them, he said, "I think you're right. But, first, I think we should talk to Mimi …"

13

"I know these emails look bad," said Dr. Emily "Mimi" Taylor, "but, I can explain ..."

"Please do," requested Robyn.

Beanie waited for Mimi to speak, but doubted she'd be able to give them a plausible reason for the emails. The electronic communication, which had taken place between Mimi and Henry weeks before Henry's murder, was suspicious.

Staring at the diminutive neurologist, Beanie recalled the exchange he'd read.

From: TAYLOR, E.

To: MONTAGUE, H.

Re: (no subject)

if you think I won't take you out, then think again.

From: MONTAGUE, H.

To: TAYLOR. E.

Re: Re: (no subject)

Is that a threat to kill me?

From: TAYLOR, E.

To: MONTAGUE, H.

Re: Re: Re: (no subject)

Not a threat, a promise.

How, Beanie wondered, was Dr. Taylor going to explain threatening to kill someone?

After a long exhale, Mimi shook her head, and said, "I have a bad temper sometimes. And when I feel bullied or marginalized, or threatened, then I lash out and say things in anger that I don't mean."

"You threatened to kill Henry because you have a bad temper?" asked Robyn.

Beanie caught the skepticism in his twin's tone, which he shared.

Mimi blinked rapidly, then pressed a finger beneath her eye to catch a tear before it fell. "I threatened Henry because he threatened me."

"Threatened you how?" asked Beanie.

Shuddering slightly, Mimi said, "Henry asked me if I wanted to invest in his Aerie Island's practice, and I told him I was interested. He told me that he and his other partners wanted to offer more services. He asked me for ten thousand dollars as an initial payment to buy into the partnership, which I gave him. But then I changed my mind."

"Why?" asked Robyn.

Her gaze somewhat defiant, Mimi said, "Because I was advised not to go into business with Henry. I was told that he would not invest my money. That he was trying to scam me."

"Who told you that?" asked Beanie.

"Dr. Liz Adams," said Mimi.

"Are you serious?" Robyn glared at Mimi. "Liz told you Henry was trying to scam you? And you believed her? Mimi, you know that Liz is a lying psycho. She hated Henry because he dumped her. Any chance she got, she was saying terrible things about him."

Beanie glanced at his sister, bothered by her defense of a man who hadn't been completely honest with her. Robyn had expressed her distrust of Henry and yet she disputed the idea that Henry might be a con artist.

Mimi said, "Liz told me that Henry tried to scam her. He asked her to invest in the cardiac center, and she did, but then she learned Henry had used the money to pay off some gambling debts, or something."

"Gambling debts?" Robyn scoffed, rolling her eyes. "Henry didn't gamble."

"Maybe he did, maybe he didn't," said Mimi. "The point is, he lied to Liz about how he used her money. When she told me that, I asked Henry for my money back, but he refused to give it to me."

Arms crossed, Robyn said, "And then you threatened to kill him?"

Shaking her head, Mimi said, "No, it wasn't like that—"

"You sent an email to Henry telling him you would take him out," said Robyn.

Beanie said, "Sounds like you wanted him dead."

"Did you kill Henry?" demanded Robyn, glaring at Mimi.

"Oh my God, no," cried Mimi. "I didn't kill Henry. I would never kill anyone. I am a doctor. I took an oath to first do no harm and I took that oath seriously. Yes, I was angry that Henry refused to return my money, but … when I said I would take Henry out, I didn't mean I would kill him."

"Then what did you mean?" asked Beanie.

Mimi sighed, dragging both hands down the side of her face. "I meant I would call the police and tell them he'd scammed me out of ten thousand dollars. I wanted him to get scared and return my money."

"But he didn't," guessed Beanie.

Mimi shook her head. "Henry said the money was gone. He'd already used it."

Robyn said, "So you killed him."

"I did not kill Henry!" insisted Mimi.

Standing, Robyn said, "Well, that's for the police to decide."

"The police?" Mimi's face went white. "You're going to show those emails to the cops? You can't do that!"

"Why not?" asked Robyn.

"Because …" Mimi sputtered for a moment, then after a ragged breath said, "Because those words need to be put in the proper context!"

"I think your words speak for themselves," said Robyn, walking toward the door.

Beanie rose to his feet.

"Please tell Robyn not to go to the police," implored Mimi. "I know the emails make me look suspicious but I didn't kill Henry. I swear I didn't!"

Saying nothing, Beanie hurried out of the office, following Robyn. His twin sister was halfway down the corridor, striding purposefully toward the elevators.

"Robyn, wait …" Beanie caught up with her, grabbing her arm. "Hold on a minute."

Pulling her arm from his grasp, Robyn said, "Hold on for what?"

"What are you going to do with those emails?"

"Are you seriously asking me that?" Robyn made a fist and banged on the elevator's down button. "I'm taking them to the police. I'm giving them to Janvier. He needs a suspect. I'm giving him someone to investigate."

The elevator doors opened. He and Robyn stepped inside. Thankful the car was empty, Beanie said, "Are you sure you want to do that?"

"Why wouldn't I?" Robyn pressed the Lobby button. "Mimi killed Henry. I know she did. And for what? Ten thousand dollars. Was that all his life was worth to her?"

Beanie sighed. "You don't know that Mimi killed Henry. Those emails don't prove murder."

"She threatens to take Henry out," Robyn said.

"The emails show that Mimi and Henry had beef," said Beanie. "So, they show a potential motive. But, Mimi can explain it as a misunderstanding. The cops will need to prove that Mimi had means and opportunity, as well."

"Well, motive is a good place to start," said Robyn as the elevator doors opened.

Walking alongside his sister through the lobby, Beanie said, "But Mimi is your friend."

"My friend who killed my boyfriend," said Robyn.

"Why don't you let me check it out before you go to the cops," suggested Beanie as they walked through the vestibule and out of the hospital. "If I can determine means and opportunity for Mimi, then we'll take the emails to the police."

Crossing the parking lot, Robyn said, "Why don't you want me to go to the police?"

"It's not that I don't want you to go to the cops," said Beanie. "I just don't want you to give the emails to Janvier because he won't investigate them. He'll declare Mimi guilty, and what if she's not?"

As they approached Beanie's SUV, Robyn said, "Janvier will jump to conclusions. But maybe the other detective will be more objective. What's his name?"

"Allen Green," said Beanie. "I'd much rather work with him. He actually takes my calls and doesn't mind giving me a comment. I can reach out to him about the emails and see what he thinks."

Exhaling, Robyn nodded. "That's a good idea."

Standing near the back of the SUV, Beanie said, "Look, I know it was probably a shock to find out about this failed business deal between Henry and Mimi—"

"That's not why I got so upset with her," said Robyn.

"It's not?"

Robyn shook her head, looking away from him. "I mean, the emails were shocking, but people keep secrets, right? You know that better than I do."

Beanie took a deep breath and decided to forgo a scathing reply. What was the point in sparring with his sister? They could trade hurtful barbs all afternoon, but what would it accomplish? Beanie wasn't surprised by Robyn's dig at his wife. His sister would always be bothered by his marriage to a former PC-5 member.

"I'm sorry. I shouldn't have said that," said Robyn, rubbing her eyes. "But I believe Mimi. She does have a temper sometimes. I've overheard her lash out at colleagues."

"Then why did you get upset with Mimi?"

"Displaced anger," said Robyn. "I'm worried about a letter I got a few days ago. It was from a lawyer representing Henry's estate. Henry left me something in his will."

Beanie was shocked. "He did?"

Robyn nodded. "I have no idea what it could be. The lawyer wouldn't tell me over the phone. I have to meet with him."

"When?"

"Day after tomorrow," said Robyn. "I'm nervous and worried. I knew Henry for seven months. So why would he leave me something in his will? And what did he leave me?"

14

"Robyn's meeting with the lawyer today about Henry's will, right?" asked Noelle as she scrambled eggs for breakfast.

Leaning against the counter in front of the sink, Beanie took a sip of coffee. "The appointment is at eleven this morning. She's going to call me when it's over and I'm gonna go over to her place so she can tell me what happened."

Noelle asked, "What do you think Henry left her?"

"I'm not sure," said Beanie, swiping a goat sausage patty from the platter next to the stove. "I wish he hadn't left her anything. I hope whatever he willed to her won't cause problems for my sister."

"What kind of problems?"

"Problems Robyn doesn't need to deal with," said Beanie. "I'm worried that Henry could have left Robyn something which will make her look like a suspect."

Noelle stirred eggs with the wooden spatula. "You mean like a large amount of money."

Beanie sighed. "If Henry left her a million dollars or something else of significant value, then that's all Janvier will need to jump to the conclusion that Robyn killed Henry for his money."

"Maybe Janvier would see that as a motive for murder," Noelle added fluffy scrambled eggs to the platter of goat sausage, then took the skillet to the sink. "But he's got to prove means and opportunity, right?"

"Babe, we're talking about Janvier." Beanie took another sip of coffee, even though the caffeine would exacerbate his already frayed nerves. "All he needs is motive."

Glancing over her shoulder at him, Noelle said, "But Detective Green is working the case with him, so maybe he'll keep Janvier in check."

Beanie walked to the kitchen table, pulled out a chair, and sat down. "I hope so."

Noelle joined him at the table. "You gave Det. Green the emails between Henry and Robyn's friend, Mimi, right?"

"He thanked me and said he would investigate," said Beanie. "But he hasn't gotten back to me."

"Well, it's only been two days," said Noelle. "He's probably doing a thorough investigation, which is a good thing, right?"

"I guess ..." Beanie finished his coffee.

Noelle made a face. "What do you mean, you guess? You don't want the cops jumping to conclusions, right?"

Beanie said, "This is going to sound horrible, but I sometimes wish Janvier would latch on to some suspect—someone who's not my sister—and then doggedly pursue that person as Henry's killer. Then I wouldn't have to worry about him coming after Robyn."

"Babe ..." Noelle reached out and grabbed Beanie's hand. "Stop worrying about Janvier suspecting Robyn. There's no evidence tying her to Henry's murder. Now, can you set the table while I go and wake up your sons?"

After Noelle left the kitchen, Beanie stood and crossed to the overhead cabinets.

Guilt washed over him. Noelle didn't understand why he was so worried about Janvier fingering Robyn for Henry's murder. His wife didn't know about Henry's dying words. *Robyn ... shot me.* No one knew. Beanie hadn't even told Robyn.

After removing the breakfast plates, Beanie walked back to the table.

He didn't like keeping a potentially devastating secret, but he had to. For now, at least. For as long as it took him to determine the validity and veracity of Henry's statement. Once he determined that Henry's words couldn't hurt Robyn, he would come clean.

15

"Henry gave you a letter?"

Beanie stared at his sister, sitting on the couch in the living room of the townhouse.

Clutching an envelope, Robyn nodded. "And this townhouse ..."

Nodding, Beanie fought disappointment. He'd prayed Robyn wouldn't receive anything expensive. He'd hoped she'd get some cheap, sentimental trinket. Instead, Henry had willed her a gorgeous bay front townhouse. A generous inheritance. The place was probably worth close to a million dollars. Now he had to pray that Janvier wouldn't think Robyn had killed Henry to get his house.

"But the letter is more important."

Sitting in the chair adjacent to the couch, Beanie asked, "What does it say?"

Robyn held the envelope toward Beanie.

Beanie opened the envelope, pulled out the letter, and read it. Frowning, he read the three lines of text once more. And then again.

Robyn if you are reading this letter then you should get the laptop from my office at the hospital and give it to the PIIBs. They should open file 13. It will tell them who killed me.

Beanie glanced at Robyn. "Is this real?"

Robyn pinched the bridge of her nose. "It must be, don't you think?"

"Did the lawyer know about the letter?"

"He hadn't read it," said Robyn, leaning back against the couch cushions. "He told me to read it after I left his office, so I did. But I can't believe it."

Beanie couldn't, either. He skimmed the letter one last time then returned it to the envelope.

Robyn said, "I just feel so horrible because I didn't believe Henry when he told me he'd bought the gun to protect himself from Liz Adams, but he *was* telling the truth. He knew Liz was going to kill him."

Beanie said, "I wonder why he didn't just tell you that in the letter. Better yet, why not send a letter to the cops himself."

"The letter says the cops need to open file thirteen," said Robyn. "That makes me think there's some evidence Henry wanted the police to see. Maybe some tangible proof that Liz killed him. Proof she wouldn't be able to deny."

"We need to get the laptop to the police," said Beanie, standing. "Where is it?"

Robyn exhaled. "I don't know."

Beanie frowned. "The letter says the laptop was in Henry's office at the hospital."

"The hospital already sent over everything from Henry's office," said Robyn. "Some orderlies packed up everything and sent it to the townhouse in Banker's boxes."

Recalling the boxes his sister had been removing files from several days ago, Beanie said, "So that means the laptop should be here."

"Right," agreed Robyn. "But it isn't."

Beanie didn't understand. "Are you sure?"

"The hospital delivered four boxes," said Robyn. "I checked all four before you got here. Twice."

"Maybe the hospital forgot to deliver some boxes," suggested Beanie.

"That's what I was thinking," said Robyn.

Beanie said, "Let's head over there."

An hour later, standing in Henry's old office on the third floor of St. Killian General, Beanie's disappointment matched his twin sister's downcast expression.

After one of the hospital security guards, a friend of Robyn's, opened the office for them, Beanie knew they weren't going to find any boxes that hadn't been delivered. The spacious office was empty. Only a large desk, a waist-high bookshelf, and two leather chairs remained. Both the desk and the bookshelf were empty. The walls and floor bare.

"This doesn't make sense," said Robyn. "If the laptop wasn't in the Banker's boxes sent to the townhouse and if it wasn't accidentally left in his office, then … where is it?"

Beanie had a thought. "Maybe we should check lost and found. Or maybe your friend in IT might know something. If the orderlies forgot the laptop, then someone in the cleaning crew might have found it and turned it in?"

Exhaling, Robyn nodded. "That's a good idea. And you know what? If it's a hospital-issued laptop, then maybe they can track the location."

Beanie said, "I think—"

Two quick, sharp knocks startled Beanie. As he looked toward the open door, a woman in pale pink scrubs—the color assigned to nurses' aides—stepped into the office.

"Hey, Rhea," greeted Robyn, stepping toward the woman. After a quick embrace, Robyn said, "Roland, this is Assistant Nurse Rhea Calais. Rhea, this is my brother—"

"Roland Bean," said the assistant nurse, holding out a hand. "You work for the *Palmchat Gazette*, don't you?"

Nodding, Beanie gave the woman a quick smile as he shook her hand, which was calloused, with a powerful grip.

"Robyn, girl, what are you doing here?" asked Rhea. "Thought you were taking some days off?"

"I'll be back in a few days to finish my classes," said Robyn. "I stopped by to make sure that all of Henry's things were boxed up and sent to his house."

"Far as I know they were," said the assistant nurse. "Well, they were until they had to be unboxed."

"Why were they unboxed?" asked Beanie, shooting a glance at Robyn.

"Was something accidentally left behind?" Robyn asked.

Lips pursed, Assistant Nurse Calais said, "No, honey. The boxes had to be reopened because Dr. Liz Adams made a stink."

"What kind of stink?" asked Robyn.

"Honey, that woman is a pill-and-a-half," said Rhea. "The orderlies had just gotten everything boxed up and then here she comes marching down the corridor like she owns the place. She claimed that something—and she never would say what—that belonged to her was in Henry's office and had been boxed up with his things. So she demanded that the orderlies open the boxes so she could look through them."

"Dr. Adams went through the boxes of Henry's things before they were sent to his townhouse?" asked Beanie, contemplating the ramifications of the psycho ex-girlfriend's actions.

"Did she find what she was looking for?" asked Robyn.

"Girl, I don't know," said Rhea. "She made the orderlies take the boxes to her office so she could look through them. I'm not sure what happened after that."

Robyn asked, "Do you know which orderlies boxed up Henry's things?"

Rhea frowned. "I think one of them was Errol White."

"Is he working today?" asked Beanie.

"I think so," said Rhea. "You need me to page him."

Robyn nodded. "Please …"

Rhea asked, "What's going on? You think something was missing from one of the boxes?"

"Some of Henry's personal items weren't in the boxes," said Robyn. "I just want to ask the orderlies if they packed those items."

Rhea scoffed. "Honey, I'll tell you what: if something is missing from those boxes, I'll bet you that Dr. Liz Adams took it …"

Orderly Errol White met Beanie and Robyn in a secluded hallway near the supply room where he'd been doing inventory.

After Robyn explained about items missing from Henry's boxes of personal effects, Beanie asked about Dr. Adams' request to have the boxes reopened.

Orderly White sneered when he said, "Dr. Adams gets on my nerves. We had just finished securing the boxes with masking tape when she showed up, yelling, and shouting. Demanding that we open the boxes. Accusing us of putting stuff in Dr. Montague's boxes that didn't belong to him."

Beanie asked, "So you opened the boxes for her?"

Orderly White said, "She demanded that we take the boxes to her office so she could look through them, so we did. And then when she was finished, she resealed the boxes and told us to come and get them."

Robyn asked, "Errol, do you remember if you packed a laptop in one of the boxes before Dr. Adams demanded that they be reopened."

Nodding, Errol said, "Well, I didn't pack it. Orderly Sampson boxed it up. I remember because we argued about whether it should be wrapped in bubble wrap or packing peanuts."

"And was the laptop still in the box after Dr. Adams looked through it?" Beanie asked.

Orderly White shrugged. "I'm guessing it was. Like I said, Dr. Adams resealed the boxes after she looked for her stuff. And we didn't reopen the boxes after she'd resealed them."

Beanie glanced at Robyn. The suspicion on his sister's face told him his twin was thinking the same thing he was thinking. Assistant Nurse Rhea had been right. Whatever was missing from the box had been taken by Dr. Liz Adams.

Following the conversation with Orderly White, Beanie and Robyn entered an elevator and headed to the lobby.

Robyn said, "Liz stole Henry's laptop. She's the only one who could have taken it out of the box after Orderly Sampson packed it. But why would she take it?"

Rubbing his jaw, Beanie said, "Henry's letter says the identity of his killer is in a file on that laptop. So, if Liz stole it, then maybe—"

"Oh my God … " Robyn stared at him. "Liz must know about the evidence in file thirteen. She doesn't want the cops to find it. She knows that if they do, they'll know that she killed Henry …"

16

"I'm sorry, sir, but Dr. Adams is not available at the moment," said the receptionist. "Would you like to leave a message?"

Fighting frustration, Beanie said, "I already left a message yesterday. And the day before that. And Dr. Adams still has not returned my calls."

"I'm sorry, sir, but Dr. Adams is very busy," said the receptionist.

Beanie drummed his fingers against the desk in his tiny cubicle at the *Palmchat Gazette* offices. "Have you been giving Dr. Adams my messages?"

"Yes, sir, I have given her your messages," said the receptionist. "I always give her all her messages."

He squeezed the receiver in a death grip. "Did you tell her that it was important that I speak with her as soon as possible?"

"Yes, sir, I did."

"Did you tell her that I need to speak with her about the death of Dr. Henry Montague?"

"I did relay that message to her, sir."

"And what did she say?"

"Dr. Adams will return your call as soon as she's able to, sir," said the receptionist. "However, she is very busy, and—"

"Thank you for your time." Beanie slammed the phone down.

Pinching the bridge of his nose, he exhaled and counted to ten under his breath. When that did nothing to calm him, he counted to twenty. And then to fifty. He kept counting until he realized no amount of counting was going to bring his blood pressure down.

Beanie leaned back in his chair and stared at the faint water stains on the ceiling tiles.

Why was he upset that Dr. Liz Adams was avoiding his calls? Hadn't he known the woman would refuse to talk to him? Three days had passed since he and Robyn had determined that Dr. Adams most likely had stolen Henry's laptop, which contained a file that he'd wanted the PIIBs to have. A file that identified his killer.

Upon realizing that Liz had taken Henry's laptop, Robyn had wanted to confront the woman. Beanie had agreed. However, Dr. Adams hadn't been at the hospital that day. Her nurse had informed them that Dr. Adams was filling in for another doctor on the island of St. Luca.

Convenient, Beanie had thought, but possible.

The health care system in the Palmchat Islands was generally good, particularly on the more prosperous islands. However, St. Luca, the poorest island, lacked the medical facilities and the doctors needed to adequately care for its citizens. Often, doctors and nurses from St. Killian General Hospital traveled to St. Luca to help meet local medical needs.

Nevertheless, Beanie believed the woman could find time to talk to him —if she wanted to.

Robyn's efforts to contact Dr. Adams had failed, so far. Henry's psycho ex-girlfriend was even less likely to return Robyn's calls, but his sister was relentless. She was determined to confront Liz about Henry's laptop and was willing to stalk the woman if she had to.

Beanie didn't plan to go that far.

However, he had contacted Det. Allen Green to inform him about Henry's laptop. Det. Green had been cordial and grateful, but Beanie wasn't sure if the man had taken him seriously. Admittedly, a letter from beyond the grave indicating that the killer's identity could be found in a file on a laptop, which happened to be missing, was somewhat farfetched. But Det. Green had agreed to check it out. As he'd agreed to look into Dr. Mimi Taylor. Beanie supposed all he could ask was for the detective's consideration. But he suspected the man might be placating him.

Beanie glanced at his watch and stood. Almost three o'clock. A good enough time for his third cup of coffee, he figured.

In the breakroom, a bright, spacious area with walls made of glass, Beanie ambled toward the coffee bar and grabbed a 12-ounce paper cup.

"Hey, how's it going?"

Recognizing the bubbly, carefree voice of Sophie Carter, a fellow reporter, Beanie turned. Followed by Stevie Bishop, another *Palmchat Gazette* journalist, Sophie bounded into the breakroom, laughing, and joking with Stevie.

"It's going," said Beanie, placing a K-cup in the Keurig machine.

"What are you working on?" asked Stevie, heading to the stainless-steel refrigerator. Opening the door, he reached in and pulled out a bottle of sparkling water.

"Fact-checking. Revisions."

"Revisions are the worst," grumbled Sophie, picking through the various K-cup flavors from the bin between the two coffee machines.

After his coffee was ready, Beanie added a bit of cream and sugar then joined Stevie at a table near the rear of the room. Minutes later, Sophie took the chair across from them and launched into a litany of complaints about how she wasn't getting enough good stories to cover. Beanie understood where she was coming from. When he'd first started at the paper, he'd been idealistic, eager to tell stories that would expose and engage and excite and empower. Instead, he'd spent his first year covering boring town hall meetings and fact-checking articles, most of them written by Caleb Olivier, the cranky curmudgeon who berated and belittled his efforts.

"You gotta make your own headlines," said Beanie. "And you have to be willing to listen and learn."

Sophie rolled her eyes. "Clichés and coffee. An afternoon delight."

Beanie laughed. "I'm serious."

Stevie said, "You don't have anything to worry about, Sophie. Viv and Leo like you."

"He's right," said Beanie. "They think you have a lot of potential. What you lack, at times, is patience."

"Can I help it if I don't want to wait around for my big break?" asked Sophie.

"Sometimes you gotta make your own breaks," said Beanie. "Remember that story I did on the engineer who was decapitated? After I came from the crime scene, I talked to Viv about it, asked her for advice on framing the story and talking to potential witnesses, and she saw my initiative and pretty much let me have the story."

"Sex, lies, and electricity," said Stevie, admiration in his tone as he nodded.

"You know," said Sophie, brown eyes flashing with excitement. "I've been thinking I should become part of the story."

Stevie frowned. "Become part of the story?"

"Like Beanie did." Sophie took a quick sip of coffee. "You were there when the cardiologist stumbled into the middle of the road and you discovered he'd been shot."

"Don't remind me," said Beanie, trying not to think about the night Henry died.

"You were part of the story, Beanie," said Sophie. "So you were assigned the story."

"How are you gonna be part of the story if you don't know when there's going to be a story?" asked Stevie.

Shrugging, Sophie said, "Obviously, it will have to happen organically. I was thinking that I might be at the bank one day and some guys might come in and rob it. Vivian will have to assign the story to me."

"Assuming that you're alive to write it and you weren't shot by the bank robbers," said Stevie.

Sophie rolled her eyes at him.

Beanie said, "You don't want to be part of the story, trust me. Especially if the victim is your sister's boyfriend."

"How is your sister?" asked Sophie.

Sighing, Beanie said, "She says she's okay, but I don't know. I think she might be having a hard time, but she doesn't want me to worry."

"Do the cops know who killed Dr. Montague?" asked Stevie.

"No viable suspects, so far," lamented Beanie.

"What about Dr. Emily Taylor?" asked Sophie. "You told Det. Green about her, right?"

Taking a sip of coffee, Beanie nodded. "He's looking into the emails between her and Henry. But I haven't heard anything from him about it. In the meantime, I gave him another suspect."

"Who?" asked Stevie.

Beanie told his co-workers about Dr. Liz Adams, Henry's letter, and the missing laptop.

"So you think the psycho ex who crashed the party killed Dr. Montague?" asked Sophie.

Rubbing his jaw, Beanie said, "It's possible. She stole Henry's laptop. She must have known there was a file on the laptop that would identify her as the killer."

Sophie said, "She's probably erased the evidence against her by now."

Stevie said, "Even if she did, my cousin could probably recover it."

Stevie's cousin, a mysterious hacker who, so far, had remained anonymous, had assisted several *Palmchat Gazette* reporters by uncovering passwords and retrieving digital data.

"What if Dr. Adams destroys the laptop?" challenged Sophie, eyes narrowed.

"Data is never really destroyed," said Stevie. "It's all out there somewhere. You just have to know how to find it."

Shrugging, Beanie said, "Well, my sister and I have both been trying to contact Dr. Adams, but she's not—"

Beanie's cell phone buzzed, interrupting him. He pulled out his phone and checked the text message he'd received. *Mr. Bean, it's Det. Green. Can you give me a call when you get a moment? Thanks.*

"Guys, it's Det. Green," said Beanie, standing.

"Maybe he's got news about a suspect in Dr. Montague's murder," said Sophie.

Nodding, Beanie said, "That's what I'm hoping."

Minutes later, back at his desk, Beanie called Det. Green.

Following quick greetings, the detective got to the point. "First of all, I again want to thank you and your sister for the information regarding doctors Taylor and Adams. I want to assure you that Det. Janvier and I are investigating those angles, but the case has taken a turn."

Beanie's gut twisted. "What kind of turn?"

"Officer Fields told me you're pretty good about keeping your sources anonymous …"

"Absolutely," said Beanie, though he wasn't concerned about writing an article about Henry's murder at the moment. He was worried about the turn in the case. Had Janvier come to the ridiculous conclusion that Robyn was a suspect?

Det. Green said, "Det. Janvier and I are looking into a connection between Dr. Montague and the PC-5."

The relief that flooded Beanie was quickly overtaken by curiosity. "You think the PC-5 had something to do with Henry's death?"

"It's possible," said Det. Green, "considering what we've found out."

"Which is what?" asked Beanie.

"Dr. Montague was a PC-5 mob doctor."

17

"Wait a minute. Henry was working for the PC-5?" asked Noelle as she crossed the bedroom, heading to the wardrobe. "Are you serious?"

As his wife's frown deepened, Beanie regretted mentioning the dreaded island gang.

Conversations with Noelle about the PC-5 could be difficult, fractious. Talking about the island gang with his wife was tricky. Like navigating a land mine. One wrong step and things could blow up in his face. There was always the potential for misunderstandings and hurt feelings. Noelle harbored guilt and trauma from her participation in the gang. Despite escaping the cartel and reinventing herself into a productive member of society, his wife wondered if she would ever truly escape her past. Many people in the Palmchat islands doubted if a former gang member could be rehabilitated. As a result, Noelle worried that her cartel ties would always be held against her. To allay her fears and calm her worries, Beanie avoided, as much as possible, the subject of the PC-5.

Clearing his throat, Beanie said, "According to Detective Green, Nico Lecrae's father is one of Henry's patients."

His wife gaped at him. "Nico Lecrae?"

Nico Lecrae was the leader of the Papillion family, the faction of the PC-5 that controlled and directed criminal operations in St. Killian. The cartel leader was as ruthless and deadly as he was charming and—according to some women—good-looking. Beanie loathed the man. More so because Lecrae had saved Noelle's life—when Beanie couldn't.

Propped up on the pillows stacked against the headboard, Beanie said, "Green told me that Henry treated Papa Lecrae for angina. And he performed everything from routine check-ups to emergency surgical procedures for other gang members, as well. The Aerie Islands facility was basically a mob clinic."

"You think it's really true?" asked Noelle, grabbing a night gown from the wardrobe.

"It's definitely true," said Beanie. "I talked to Lime Shoes. Stopped by the Purple Gecko before I came home."

Noelle made a face. "I wish you didn't have to deal with him."

"He's a good source."

"He's a PC-5 gang member, which makes him dangerous and unpredictable," said Noelle, slipping the night gown over her head. "And I know I was once in the cartel, so I have no right to judge, but ..."

"Babe, if it makes you feel better," said Beanie. "I think he kind of likes me."

"He likes you?" Noelle scoffed. "Beanie, he didn't agree to be your source because he likes the way you write. He's trying to control the narrative when it comes to the cartel. Don't forget, Lime Shoes is the guy who kidnapped you—"

"I wouldn't say he kidnapped me," disputed Beanie.

Noelle frowned. "The man had his thugs grab you, blindfold you, throw you in the back of a car and drive you to an undisclosed location so he could warn you not to write bad things about the cartel."

Beanie said, "Actually, he warned me not to print unsubstantiated assumptions and uncorroborated conclusions about the cartel. They don't mind if I print the truth. The cartel just doesn't want to be associated with crimes they didn't commit."

Noelle exhaled, shaking her head. "Fine. Whatever. What did Lime Shoes tell you?"

"He confirmed what Det. Green told me," said Beanie. "Henry was a mob doctor. He borrowed money from the cartel."

Noelle walked to the foot of the bed. "Why?"

"Henry has been sued several times for medical malpractice," said Beanie. "I'm going to research the cases when I go into work tomorrow. Anyway, he reached settlements so he wouldn't lose his license. But these settlements were in the millions. People died because of his incompetence. Henry couldn't pay back the cartel."

Noelle scoffed. "No one can ever pay back the cartel. They design it that way. Once you become indebted to them, they force you into indentured servitude."

Beanie nodded. "To settle his debt with the PC-5, the cartel made him an offer, which he couldn't refuse. And that's how he became a mob doctor."

Noelle asked, "So, the cops think the PC-5 killed Henry?"

Beanie said, "Det. Green said he and Janvier are thinking Henry became the doctor who knew too much and had to be silenced, so the cartel killed him. Or maybe Henry found out something and tried to use the information to blackmail the cartel."

Shaking her head, Noelle said, "They're wrong."

"How can you be so sure?"

His wife gave him a look. "Have you forgotten who my father is?"

An icy chill passed through Beanie. He didn't like to think about Noelle's father. Josue Chartres. Notorious island hitman. Ruthless enforcer of the cartel's dreaded "Death List". People who worked to dismantle and destroy the cartel were placed on the list. Noelle's father, who'd been jailed years ago and was currently spending the rest of his life in prison, had been the PC-5's deadliest executioner.

"When the PC-5 sends someone to kill you," said Noelle, crawling onto the bed and cuddling next to him, "you don't end up shot haphazardly and staggering in the middle of the road. Henry's murder was not a cartel hit."

Rubbing his jaw, Beanie glanced at the ceiling. "That's what Lime Shoes said. He also told me the cartel had no reason to kill Henry. The arrangement was working fine."

Noelle said, "I think one of the doctors killed Henry."

"I think you might be right," said Beanie. "Question is, which one? Dr. Liz Adams? Or Dr. Mimi Taylor?"

18

"Where did you find this file?" asked Beanie.

Robyn exhaled as she paced around the living room. "I told you. I was cleaning out Henry's home office and I remembered that one of his desk drawers has a false bottom."

Beanie stared at the blue file folder Robyn had shoved at him the moment he'd arrived at the Adagio Bay townhouse Henry had willed to her. Beanie had been driving home from a long, boring day of dull stories and tedious fact-checking when he'd received his sister's frantic text. *Found something you need to see. Can u come over now?* Beanie had hesitated. He'd been heading to his mother-in-law's house to get the boys, and then head home, but he agreed to her request.

"What's in the file?" asked Beanie.

"I don't know," said Robyn, wrapping her arms around herself as she strode from one end of the living area to the other. "I didn't want to look until you got here. I'm nervous. I don't want to look. And yet, I do want to look. But, if I look then I can't un-look. Guess I'm afraid to look."

"Why?" asked Beanie.

Robyn stopped pacing to gape at him. "How can you ask me that? Didn't you tell me that Det. Green said Henry was a mob doctor? What if that file contains some evidence against the PC-5? Something Henry shouldn't have had. Evidence that could put me on the Death List if the cartel finds out I have it."

"I don't think you have to be afraid to look in this file," said Beanie. "Remember I told you Lime Shoes said that the arrangement between Henry and the cartel was amicable. I don't think Henry was trying to collect evidence against the mob. He was too busy trying to pay off his debts."

Exhaling, Robyn resumed her pacing. "I can't believe he borrowed money from the PC-5. What was he thinking?"

Beanie said, "I think he was desperate to pay those malpractice settlements."

"And don't remind me about those malpractice settlements," said Robyn. "On second thought—weren't you supposed to look up the cases?"

Sighing, Beanie said, "Turns out Henry made a number of surgical mistakes. There were also some deadly misdiagnoses. Those petitions were disturbing and scary."

Robyn pinched the bridge of her nose. "I don't even know what to think, you know? Except maybe, I sure can pick 'em, right? How could I have been so wrong about Henry? How could I have not seen the warning signs?"

"Were there warning signs?" asked Beanie.

Robyn shrugged and joined him on the couch, flopping down on the cushion. "There must have been, don't you think? But I didn't want to see them. I wanted so bad to be in a relationship. To be in love. To find the one."

Beanie reached forward and placed the file on the coffee table. "Was Henry the one?"

With a laughing scoff, Robyn said, "Henry wasn't even close to being the one."

"He wasn't?" asked Beanie.

Robyn shook her head. "Nope."

"Did you love him?"

"I wanted to," said Robyn. "I liked him. He was charming and sexy, but … other than that …"

"How did he feel about you?" asked Beanie. "Was he in love with you?"

"I doubt it," said Robyn.

"Are you sure? He left you his townhouse," pointed out Beanie.

"Which I'm probably going to have to sell," said Robyn. "Turns out, Henry had taken out a third mortgage on the place."

"That's a shame," said Beanie. "It is a nice townhouse."

Robyn sighed. "Okay, we've delayed the inevitable long enough. Open the file."

Beanie grabbed the file and flipped it open.

"What's in it?"

Frowning, Beanie said, "More emails between Henry and Mimi."

"Yet another thing I didn't know about Henry," said Robyn. "His relationship with Mimi. When I introduced the two of them, they acted like they hardly knew each other."

After reading the email, Beanie said, "I don't know how well they knew each other but there is one thing Henry knew about Mimi."

"What's that?"

Beanie closed the file and passed it to his sister. "Take a look."

Her expression cautious, Robyn received the file as though it was toxic, then opened it. "The first email is from Mimi … she writes: *Okay, so you know the truth about me. Now what?* Then Henry replies: *Now you pay me to keep my mouth shut.*"

Beanie said, "Henry was blackmailing Mimi."

Robyn said, "Oh my God … Henry wrote: *You're not really a doctor. You don't have a license to practice medicine anymore but you're pretending to be a licensed physician, putting patients in danger.* Mimi replied: *Just because I don't have a license doesn't mean I'm not a good doctor!* Henry wrote: *not interested in debating your medical skills. First payment due by end of week.*"

"Henry demanded ten thousand dollars from Mimi," said Beanie.

Robyn said, "And he told her he was going to the hospital board if she didn't pay him. That ten thousand dollar check I found wasn't for an investment in Henry's practice."

"It was hush money," said Beanie.

"That's why she threatened to kill Henry," said Robyn, jumping up from the couch. "She didn't want her money back. She was tired of Henry blackmailing her."

"Exactly," said Beanie. "We need to give the emails to Detective—"

"Did you read this one?"

"What one?"

"This second email in the file," said Robyn, holding the document toward him.

Beanie took it, and read the messages.

From: MAGENTA FLOWER
    To: MONTAGUE, H.
    Re: (no subject)
I don't have any more money to give you

From: MONTAGUE, H.
    To: MAGENTA FLOWER
    Re: Re: (no subject)
You better find some or you're going to jail. You got a nice Rolex watch. I can take that as collateral

From: MAGENTA FLOWER
    To: MONTAGUE, H.
    Re: (no subject)
I can't give you that watch. My father gave that to me before he passed away. A present for graduation

From: MONTAGUE, H.
    To: MAGENTA FLOWER
    Re: Re: (no subject)
Not interested in your sob story. I'll take the watch or the cash. It's up to you

Beanie glanced at Robyn. "Who is … Magenta Flower? Is that Mimi?"

Robyn said, "Has to be. Probably a secret email she used to contact Henry."

"But she used her real email address in the other emails," Beanie pointed out.

Shrugging, Robyn said, "She probably realized she was incriminating herself by using her real email."

Nodding, Beanie said, "So, Henry demanded Mimi's Rolex watch."

"That's so awful," said Robyn, sinking onto the couch again. "Henry was so awful. An incompetent cardiologist responsible for the death of several of his patients. A cartel doctor. A blackmailer ... "

"I don't like to speak ill of the dead and I think it's wrong to blame the victim," said Beanie, "but—"

"But Henry seems to have had it coming to him, didn't he?" Robyn sighed. "After everything I've found out about him, I'm not surprised someone killed him."

19

"Reporter Bean, this is Detective Philippi Janvier," said the detective, his voice haughty and imperial. "Do you have a moment?"

"Detective Janvier," said Beanie, trying to temper his shock as he pulled the phone from his ear to stare at it for a moment. Was Janvier really calling him? Was the detective who never returned his phone calls really on the other end of the line? "Yes, sure, I have a moment."

Beanie turned to his computer and opened a Word file. If Janvier had called to give him information about a case, which Beanie doubted, he nevertheless wanted to document the call.

"In an effort to not waste time, I will be as succinct as possible," said the detective. "Recently, you provided information to me and Detective Green concerning the murder of Dr. Henry Montague."

"Right," said Beanie. Two days ago, after learning about the emails found in Henry's secret false bottom drawer, Beanie had made copies and faxed them to Janvier and Green. Detective Green had thanked Beanie and promised to investigate the emails between Henry and Dr. Mimi Taylor. Detective Janvier had remained silent.

But now the incompetent detective had called him. Why? Did Janvier have news about Henry's murder? Had there been a break in the case? If so, Beanie doubted Janvier would share those developments with him. But, anything was possible, Beanie supposed. Which could be a problem. If anything was possible, then Janvier might be calling with bad news.

Beanie tried to ignore the sinking feeling suddenly settling over him.

"Reporter Bean, your investigative efforts are neither admirable nor amusing ... "

Beanie frowned, hands poised over his wireless keyboard. "Excuse me?"

"I realize your profession requires you to meddle in official police matters but I do not need nor do I want your assistance in solving the murder of Dr. Henry Montague."

Beanie rolled his eyes. Detective Janvier could use all the help he could get. He itched to tell the detective that if the case was solved in a timely manner, it would be because of Detective Green, but he held his tongue. No need to unnecessarily antagonize the bumbling idiot.

"I wasn't trying to meddle—"

"I do not appreciate your attempts to play amateur sleuth," said the detective.

"Amateur sleuth?" Beanie pulled the phone from his ear to look at it again.

"I must insist that you refrain from forwarding to myself and Detective Green documents and papers you've collected as part of your information gathering," said Janvier.

"Detective Janvier, with all due respect ..." Beanie paused to collect himself. The last thing Janvier deserved was respect. "I was only trying to provide crucial evidence to the police—"

"Reporter Bean, you have neither the intelligence nor the acumen to determine if the evidence is crucial, or not," huffed Janvier.

Beanie gripped the phone receiver. Had Janvier just called him stupid?

"I must advise you to leave the investigating to the professionals," said Janvier. "If you insist on sticking your nose into my investigation, I will have no choice but to arrest you for obstructing justice. Do I make myself clear?"

"Clear as mud," said Beanie, ending the call before the detective could respond with another asinine directive. He couldn't believe the unmitigated gall of the detective. But, on second thought, Beanie supposed Janvier's superiority complex didn't surprise him. The man was an inept buffoon with a string of botched investigations to his credit, and yet he viewed himself as a genius detective.

The desk phone rang again. Beanie exhaled. Probably Janvier calling back to protest Beanie's abrupt ending of their previous phone call. Glancing at the Caller-ID, Beanie paused. *BEAN, ROBYN*. Beanie's gut twisted. Why was his sister calling him on his work phone in the middle of the day? Could there be some new development in the case? Praying that nothing bad had happened, Beanie picked up the receiver. "Hey, what's up?"

"Can you stop by the townhouse tonight?' asked Robyn. "I want to talk to you about Henry's laptop."

Curious, Beanie asked, "What about it?"

Robyn said, "I think I know how to get it back from Liz Adams."

20

"You want to … what?"

Sitting across from his twin sister at the dining room table in the Adagio Bay townhouse, Beanie stared at Robyn, concerned by his sister's serious tone and the determined look on her face.

"I want to steal the laptop back from Liz," said Robyn.

"Are you serious?" asked Beanie.

"How else are we going to get the laptop?" demanded Robyn.

"Breaking the law is not the answer," said Beanie.

"Then what is the answer?" Shaking her head, Robyn said, "We have to get Henry's laptop. We need to see the evidence and give it to the police, which is what Henry wanted. Those were his wishes. I need to fulfill them."

Bummed by the sadness in his sister's gaze, Beanie reached across the table, took her hand, and squeezed it. "Don't worry, okay. We'll get the laptop."

"How?" Robyn pulled her hand away. "Liz isn't going to give it to us. She won't even return my calls."

"Maybe we need to ambush her," suggested Beanie.

"Ambush her?"

"Show up at her place out of the blue," said Beanie. "Unannounced. So she doesn't have time to stonewall us, or pretend she's helping out at a clinic in St. Luca."

"That's not going to work," said Robyn. "I don't know where Liz Adams lives."

Beanie said, "I could probably find out where—"

The doorbell rang. A series of high-pitched dings in rapid succession. One continuous cacophonous note.

Beanie frowned. "You expecting someone?"

Standing Robyn said, "No. But I'm going to find out who's trying to break the doorbell."

As his sister left the dining room and headed through the open living area to the spacious foyer, Beanie contemplated a strategy to ambush Dr. Liz Adams. The woman was avoiding him. Probably because she knew why he wanted to talk to her. She must have found out that he and Robyn had gone to the hospital searching for Henry's laptop only to be informed that Dr. Adams had searched the boxes from Henry's office. The doctor was probably aware that he and Robyn suspected she'd taken the laptop, and—

A riot of vile, angry curses filled the air.

Beanie tensed. Someone—a woman, judging from the shrill tone—was calling Robyn every name in the book, and then some. Jumping up from the table, Beanie hurried toward the foyer. His sister and Dr. Mimi Taylor stood face-to-face, fussing, and pointing fingers.

Walking into the foyer, Beanie hoped his presence would help diffuse the dangerous tension between the women. Robyn and Mimi scowled at each other, looking as though they might be ready to scratch each other's eyes out.

"I can't believe you snitched on me!" Mimi sneered at Robyn. "Can't believe you gave the police those emails Henry and I sent each other!"

"I can't believe you're practicing medicine without a license," Robyn shot back.

"Just because I no longer have a license doesn't mean I'm not a good doctor," Mimi insisted.

"Tell that to the medical board," Robyn advised, arms crossed over her chest.

"I tried to," said Mimi. "I just came back from an emergency hearing. The police gave the emails to the St. Killian General Hospital board of directors. Not only did they fire me but they are bringing charges against me!"

"As they should," said Robyn. "You put patients' lives in danger. Do you even know what 'first do no harm' means?"

"I would never hurt any of my patients," said Mimi.

"You must have," said Beanie. "Your medical license was revoked."

"Not because I hurt a patient," snipped Mimi.

"Then why did you lose your license?" asked Robyn.

"Because I had a diabetic attack," snapped Mimi.

"A diabetic attack?" echoed Beanie.

Robyn shook her head. "You have diabetes?"

Mimi sighed. "Yes, I do. The hospital I worked for at the time accused me of being intoxicated while I was assisting during a surgical procedure, but that wasn't true. I wasn't drunk. I had a diabetic episode which can mimic intoxication, but the hospital fired me because they saw me as a liability. The patient sued the hospital for allowing a surgeon with diabetes in the operating room, but I did not harm that patient! I am a good doctor, much better than Henry, with his slew of malpractice suits a mile long, and he knew that. He had no right to take advantage of my misfortune."

"A misfortune you brought on yourself," said Robyn. "If you knew your diabetes could affect your performance, you shouldn't have assisted with the operation that day."

Waving a dismissive hand, Mimi said, "Forget it. I don't expect you to understand. I thought we were friends, but obviously not. You should have come to me with the emails first instead of giving them to the police! But you decided to blow up my life and ruin my career!"

"I think you should leave now," said Robyn, extending a hand toward the door.

"I'm not leaving without my money," announced Mimi, crossing her arms.

"Your money?" Robyn shook her head.

"The ten thousand dollars Henry stole from me," Mimi said. "I want it back!"

"I don't have your ten thousand dollars," said Robyn. "Or, your Rolex, either."

Mimi frowned. "What Rolex?"

"The Rolex Henry demanded as payment," said Beanie, recalling the mention of the watch in the emails between Mimi and Henry. "It was your graduation gift."

"I don't have a Rolex," said Mimi.

"You don't?"

"No, I don't," said Mimi.

"Are you sure?" asked Beanie.

Mimi rolled her eyes. "Trust me, if I had a Rolex, I'd be pawning it right now."

Robyn said, "Henry emailed you about the Rolex."

"Wasn't me," said Mimi, as she pivoted toward the door. "Must have been someone else Henry was blackmailing."

21

Beanie took a third sip of his second cup of coffee.

He stared at his computer, skimming the story he'd been fact-checking for the past few hours. Normally, it didn't take long to make sure there was nothing libelous in his articles, but it was a slow news day. His passive scrutiny gave him the chance to reflect on a story that had sputtered out—the murder of Dr. Henry Montague.

After his follow-up article, which offered one or two additional details, there hadn't been much more to report. The police investigation appeared to have stalled. Weeks had passed and there were still no new developments. At least, there had been nothing new the cops were willing to share with him. Janvier had warned him against doing any amateur sleuthing, so Beanie didn't expect the bumbling detective to provide any updates.

Detective Green had proved to be a better source. He was willing to share information and not above checking out the tips Beanie had given him. One of which had panned out. When Beanie had forwarded the emails between Dr. Mimi Taylor and Henry to Detective Green, Beanie wasn't sure the messages would be given any credence. But Green had given the emails serious consideration. Unlike Janvier, Green had viewed the exchanges between the doctors with the appropriate suspicion. As a result, Mimi had been exposed.

Taking another sip of coffee, Beanie reflected on Mimi's contentious confrontation with Robyn.

The woman had some nerve to blame Robyn for her termination. Despite Mimi's insistence that the revocation of her license had been unjustified, she'd had no right to falsify records to continue her medical career. Beanie figured she'd decided to practice medicine on a Caribbean island where she, no doubt, believed she would get away with her crimes. She probably thought the island's governance of its health department to be inferior and unsophisticated.

Beanie suspected Mimi's story about a diabetic episode was sketchy and he'd been right. Research into the former doctor's background proved the hospital had good cause to fire her and revoke her license. The surgical team had testified to the hospital administrators that Mimi's breath reeked of alcohol. Subsequent blood tests showed Mimi didn't have diabetes. What she'd had was a blood alcohol level three times the legal limit.

Mimi's decision to practice medicine without a license was disturbing. The woman was guilty. But Beanie was more interested in her viability as a suspect in Henry's murder. Was she guilty of shooting Henry? As soon as he'd arrived at the newspaper's offices, Beanie had left a message with Detective Green concerning whether, or not, the cops liked Mimi as Henry's killer, but the detective hadn't returned his call.

Beanie stroked his jaw.

Mimi claimed no involvement in Henry's murder. Beanie wasn't sure if he believed her. An evaluation of the unlicensed doctor as a suspect showed a clear motive. Henry had been blackmailing her. He knew her secret and used it to extort money from her. Mimi's secret had been huge. Bombshell information that could blow up her life.

With a few clicks of his mouse, Beanie saved the article he'd been fact-checking to the newspaper's internal database, then emailed an attachment copy to Vivian for review.

He hoped the cops would find definitive proof that Mimi killed Henry. Or, if not Mimi, then Dr. Liz Adams. And, if not her, then … someone. Problem was, he didn't know if the cops had a definitive suspect. Someone they liked as Henry's killer. If they did, Beanie would know for sure Henry had been delusional when he'd gasped those fateful frightening words before he died. *Robin shot me.*

Beanie glanced at the computer screen until the words blurred. Why did he need the cops to name a suspect to know for sure that Henry had been delusional when he'd claimed Robyn had shot him? He didn't. Beanie chided himself for his doubts. But he didn't have doubts about Henry's confusion. He wondered why Henry had been confused. The dying man's last words were troubling. Weird. Why would Henry have said Robyn had shot him when it wasn't possible?

Beanie decided to focus on Dr. Liz Adams.

Henry's crazy ex who'd crashed the birthday party certainly had a motive. She was a scorned woman. Rejected by Henry who'd replaced her with Robyn. Beanie wondered if getting dumped could cause a person to kill. It was possible, but was it probable? After all, couples broke up. And, if he recalled correctly, most of Dr. Adams' venom had been spewed at Robyn. If Liz was going to target someone for homicidal vengeance, it would have been his sister.

Beanie finished his coffee, then tossed the paper cup in the waste basket beneath his small desk. Grabbing his desk phone, Beanie placed a call to Dr. Liz Adams. Robyn had told him Dr. Adams would be treating patients at her clinic this week. Beanie figured a surprise visit might be in order, considering the woman's pervasive avoidance, but he wanted to make sure she was actually in the office.

Before his first call to the elusive obstetrician, Beanie had googled the doctor to find out more about her private practice. She operated the Handweg Women's Center, which served low-income residents. On the website, her bio listed her as a passionate advocate for women who lived at or below the poverty line. She was concerned with women who had some of the highest rates of deaths during pregnancy. Her clinic's primary goal was providing quality pre-and-post natal care. When a photo of the women's clinic appeared on the computer screen, Beanie realized he recognized the commercial strip center where the Handweg Women's Center was sandwiched between a nail salon and a liquor store.

Beanie supposed he should find it hard to reconcile the idea that a woman dedicated to bringing life into the world could also ruthlessly plot to end a life. But he didn't. Throughout his years of covering crime and homicides, Beanie had learned that people were capable of anything. Even good doctors who cared for mothers and infants could be diabolical under certain circumstances.

"Dr. Adams, please," requested Beanie. "Tell her it's Roland Bean from the *Palmchat Gazette*."

"One moment," said the receptionist.

Beanie exhaled. Expecting to get the doctor's voice mail again, he contemplated hanging up, but decided—

"Mr. Bean, I'm very busy with patients today, so let's make this quick, shall we?"

Shocked that the doctor was on the line, Beanie said, "Fine by me."

"I guess you want to know if I killed Henry?"

"Actually, I wanted to talk to you about something else," said Beanie. "But, since you brought it up, did you kill Henry?"

"Of course, I didn't kill Henry. But I'm not surprised he's dead."

"Why is that?"

"He was an arrogant, narcissistic opportunist who didn't care about anyone but himself," she said.

"And yet you were once in love with him."

"Love is not always blind, Mr. Bean," said Dr. Adams. "Sometimes love has twenty/twenty vision."

"So, even though you thought Henry was a horrible person, you loved him anyway?"

"Exactly," said the doctor. "Which is why I didn't kill him. I loved Henry. Sure, I was upset when we broke up. I wanted to spend the rest of my life with him."

"But he'd moved on," interjected Beanie. "And you were upset about that, as well. Angry enough to crash a birthday party."

"Not my finest hour, I'll admit," said the doctor. "But, I was drunk, which isn't an excuse, merely a reason why I wasn't making the best decisions that night. And you are right, I was upset that Henry was in a new relationship."

"Maybe you were so upset that you decided if you couldn't have Henry, then no one could."

"But I could have Henry," said Dr. Adams.

Beanie frowned. "What do you mean?"

"Just because Henry and I were broken up didn't mean we weren't together."

"Are you saying—"

"Henry wasn't completely faithful to your sister," said Dr. Adams. "She was aware that he was cheating on her."

Beanie scoffed. "I doubt that. Robyn wouldn't have anything to do with a guy cheating on her."

"Mr. Bean, you'd be surprised at what women will put up with when the biological clock is ticking and the pickings are slim," said Dr. Adams. "Women get to a point in life where they don't need romance. Don't need to be wined and dined. They want a husband. Kids. If they find a guy who's willing to give them those things, then they're willing to look the other way when the guy isn't exactly Mr. Right."

Disappointment coursed through Beanie. He hated to think of his sister settling or lowering her standards. Had she ignored Henry's blatant infidelity because she'd thought he was her best chance at happily ever after? Beanie hoped not, but hadn't he harbored suspicions that Robyn had turned a blind eye to Henry's shenanigans?

"Anyway, what's this something else you wanted to talk to me about?"

Clearing his throat, Beanie said, "Henry's laptop."

There was a pause, and then Dr. Adams said, "I don't know anything about Henry's laptop."

Beanie tried a different approach. "Why did you demand to go through the boxes of Henry's things that the orderlies packed up to be sent to Robyn?"

"I was looking for something that belonged to me," she said. "Something I'd loaned to Henry.

"What?"

"Hold on … "

Beanie heard voices in the background.

Dr. Adams said, "One of my patients has gone into labor. I have to go."

The line disconnected.

Cursing under his breath, Beanie hung up the phone. He didn't believe for one minute that Liz Adams knew nothing about Henry's laptop. Like

Robyn, he was convinced the OB-GYN had stolen it, but why? Leaning back in his chair, Beanie stared at the water stains on the tiles. Before concluding that Liz had stolen Henry's laptop, Robyn had viewed Liz as a psychotic, vengeful scorned woman who wanted the cardiologist dead.

But what if jealousy hadn't been Dr. Liz Adams' motive.

Something Mimi had said came to Beanie's mind. *Must have been someone else Henry was blackmailing!*

Had Henry been blackmailing the OB-GYN? And if that was true, then she'd had good reason to steal the laptop. There must have been evidence on the laptop that incriminated her. Evidence that gave Dr. Liz Adams a motive to kill Henry.

22

"Thanks for agreeing to meet with me," said Detective Allen Green, mopping his forehead with a napkin from the Hullabaloo Coffee Shop vendor kiosk.

"No problem," said Beanie, taking a sip of his latte. Beneath an increasingly cloudy sky, he sat across from Green at the small bamboo bistro table, one of dozens positioned between towering palms. The area was designated for dining, where patrons enjoyed a meal from one of the many food trucks parked along the perimeter of the square.

Beanie had joined the detective in the long line at the popular coffee stand when he'd arrived at Pourciau Square. The detective had told him he'd be in the queue for afternoon java during their quick phone conversation half an hour ago. Beanie had been working on witness statements for his latest articles when Green had called. The detective wanted to meet, but not at the station. Beanie felt a fissure of alarm but tried to keep his tone calm and steady when he agreed to meet Green at Pourciau Square. He'd asked Green why he wanted to meet, but the detective felt it would be better if they spoke in person.

After hanging up the phone, Beanie fought panic. Wasn't sure why he was worried. Maybe because Green hadn't wanted to meet at the police station? But why would that be alarming? If anything, Beanie felt he should be reassured that the conversation would be casual. Maybe Green wanted to tell him something off the record. Janvier had insisted that Beanie be kept in the dark about any and all police investigations, so Green probably thought it would be best to converse away from the station.

Still, as Beanie walked the four blocks to Pourciau Square, he wondered why Green refused to tell him what he wanted to talk about. Why did they have to meet in person? He figured the detective had news about Henry's killer. Maybe there had been a break in the case. Maybe the cops had a suspect.

And, for reasons he didn't want to dwell on, his sister came to mind as well. *Robyn ... shot me.* Beanie didn't know why Henry had gasped those words. He had promised himself to find out, but he hadn't been able to bring himself to investigate. He'd convinced himself that he didn't need to determine the veracity of Henry's dying claim. The truth was that he didn't want to determine the veracity. And so he hadn't shared Henry's dying words with Robyn. Or Noelle. Or anyone. He'd tried his best to forget Henry's dying declaration, which couldn't have been true.

There was no way Robyn could have killed Henry.

As Robyn's brother, her twin, Beanie knew she was not capable of cold-blooded murder.

But the investigative journalist in him demanded an objective assessment of the clues and facts. And yet, he didn't think he could be objective. He couldn't methodically speculate about the possibility of his sister's involvement in the murder of her boyfriend.

Detective Green said, "I won't keep you long, but there's something you should know."

Beanie's pulse ratcheted. Telling himself the coffee had him jittery, he asked, "What's that?"

His gaze passive, and yet penetrating, Green said, "It's about your sister."

Beanie swallowed. "What about her?"

"You talked to her about the night Dr. Montague was killed, right?"

His pulse jumped, but Beanie knew it wasn't from the effects of the double espresso. Green's question bothered him. Put him on guard. It wasn't pointed. There was genuine curiosity in the man's tone, but he sensed Green was fishing. Or hunting. Looking for confirmation for a suspicion he harbored, maybe. Beanie cautioned himself not to jump to conclusions. Or think the worst.

Nodding, Beanie said, "I did."

"What did she tell you?" asked Detective Green. "Janvier questioned her, but when I looked at his case notes, there weren't many details."

"She didn't have much to say about Henry's death," said Beanie. "I mean, she didn't know anything about how he was killed, or when, or why."

"She have any idea *who* killed Dr. Montague?" asked Green. "Or, maybe who might have wanted him dead?"

"At the time of his death, Robyn told Janvier that she suspected Dr. Liz Adams," said Beanie. "She suspects Dr. Liz Adams stole Henry's laptop, which I told you about."

"And which I appreciate very much," said the detective.

"But, then she found out about his issues with Dr. Mimi Taylor. Have you been able to determine if either of the doctors killed Henry?"

"Unfortunately, I have not," admitted Detective Green. "I'm still looking into the doctors, or rather, I was …"

"But you're not anymore?"

"I plan to continue investigating the doctors," said Green. "But, Janvier wants us to focus on another person of interest."

"Who?" Beanie asked, taking another sip of coffee.

Detective Green said, "Robyn Bean."

Beanie nearly choked as he fought not to spew coffee all over the detective.

"I happen to think Janvier is completely off base," said Green.

After managing to swallow the coffee, Beanie coughed, then took a deep breath. "Janvier thinks my sister had something to do with Henry's death?"

"He won't come right out and say he suspects her of murder," said Green. "He doesn't trust your sister. He's convinced she knows more than she admitted to him, which was why I wanted to know what she'd told you."

Beanie took a deep breath. Forcing himself to focus, he glanced toward the imposing Pourciau Bank, with its massive Caribbean Colonial façade. He felt as though his worst nightmare was coming true. He'd hoped Janvier wouldn't target his sister, as he had Noelle. He'd told himself it wasn't possible. That as inept as Janvier was, even he wouldn't put two and two together and come up with Robyn as a suspect in Henry's murder. Deep down, Beanie supposed he'd secretly believed his sister would be viewed with suspicion. Unwarranted suspicion, of course.

Beanie asked "Why doesn't Janvier trust her? What does he think she didn't tell him?"

Green said, "Janvier obtained exterior video surveillance from Henry's townhouse."

His mouth going dry, Beanie again cautioned himself not to think the worst. No need to panic if he didn't have to, and why would he have to? Robyn had done nothing wrong. Nevertheless, video surveillance was worrisome. Could be problematic. Seeing was believing, after all. Video didn't lie. But, he didn't have to worry about the video. In fact, the video might be helpful. Might shed some clue as to who might have killed Henry.

"What does the video show?" asked Beanie.

Green hesitated.

Beanie's pulse jumped.

"I downloaded a copy to my phone," said Green, placing his cell on the table. "Janvier would kill me if he knew I was showing this to you, but I think you should see it …"

Staring at the phone as though it was something vile he'd stepped in, Beanie asked, "Why should I see it?"

"This video is from the night of Dr. Montague's death," said the detective, swiping and tapping the screen with his index finger.

Anxious, and against his better judgment, Beanie watched the surveillance video as Green provided narration.

"So … at 9:11 p.m., Dr. Montague exits the townhouse followed by Ms. Bean," said Green.

On the screen, Henry walked out of the apartment into the breezeway. Robyn followed him and they conversed in the breezeway.

"At 9:18 p.m., they're having a conversation," said Green. "Appears to be combative."

Beanie frowned, peering at the small screen. There was no sound but Henry and Robyn gestured animatedly. The conversation appeared intense. A heated discussion, thought Beanie. An argument, like the one they'd been having in the boys' bedroom. Robyn grabbed Henry's arm, but he yanked it away. Moments later, Henry pointed a finger in Robyn's face, which she slapped away.

"At 9:26 p.m., Dr. Montague leaves and Ms. Bean heads back inside."

On the video, Henry shook his head and left the breezeway while Robyn went back into the townhouse.

Green said, "Let me advance the video to 9:30 p.m. when Robyn exits the townhouse."

"Where did she go?" asked Beanie.

"She didn't tell you?" asked Green.

Beanie shook his head. He hadn't known to ask. Robyn hadn't mentioned anything about the argument with Henry in the breezeway.

"I'll advance the video again," said Green. "Now we're at 9:43 p.m. when Robyn returns to the townhouse."

Rubbing his jaw, Beanie wondered where his sister had gone in those thirteen minutes. Why had she left the townhouse? Had she gone after Henry? Maybe tried to find him?

"Nothing else happens on the video after 9:45 p.m.," said Green, tapping the screen to end the video. "Except that Dr. Montague doesn't return to the townhouse because he was murdered."

Beanie stared at Detective Green. "What does Janvier think about this video? Does he like Robyn for Henry's murder?"

Green shook his head. "As I said, he thinks your sister is hiding something."

"What do you think?" Beanie asked.

"The video raises questions," said Green. "And I'm sure your sister has an explanation, but the footage can be misunderstood. Or misconstrued. That's what I'm worried about. I have a feeling Janvier is going to come to the wrong conclusion based on this video."

Beanie exhaled. "The wrong conclusion being that my sister killed Henry."

"That's possible," admitted Green. "Janvier might decide that this video is a smoking gun and go after Robyn. Meanwhile, the real killer is getting away with murder."

"You don't suspect Robyn?"

"I don't believe your sister killed her boyfriend."

Relieved, Beanie asked, "You have any theories about who murdered Henry?"

"I was leaning toward Dr. Mimi Taylor," said Green. "But she has an alibi for the night Henry died."

Beanie felt something in him sink. "An alibi?"

Green nodded. "Dr. Taylor was called into the ER around nine that night. About an hour after she and her fiancé left your birthday party. There was a bad boating accident. Lots of injuries. She was at the hospital until five the next morning. As you would expect, lots of hospital video surveillance and dozens of witnesses confirm her alibi."

Beanie nodded, trying to mask his disappointment.

Detective Green said, "I do have another theory."

"What's that?"

"My money is on the PC-5," said Green. "Henry was working for the gang. I think he betrayed them, and they killed him."

23

"There's surveillance video of the night Henry died," said Beanie, glancing at his sister, sitting across from him. They shared a small table near the floor-to-ceiling plate glass windows of the Hullabaloo coffee shop, located a few blocks from the *Palmchat Gazette*.

At ten in the morning, the popular café bustled with tourists and island residents. Their muted chatter mixed with acoustic reggae music and the whirring of milk being steamed into froth.

Robyn frowned. "Surveillance video?"

"It shows you and Henry arguing in the breezeway outside the townhouse," said Beanie, deciding not to belabor the point. Walking from the newspaper's offices to the coffee shop, he'd contemplated how to broach the subject. He determined that a blunt, no-nonsense approach was best with his sister.

Beanie had texted her yesterday afternoon, immediately after his meeting with Allen Green. As the detective had walked away, Beanie stayed behind, furiously typing messages to Robyn, anxious to talk with her. His texts had gone unanswered. He'd spent the rest of the afternoon and evening worried and distracted, alternating between moments of blind panic and rational calm.

One moment, he was convinced his sister's arrest was imminent. The next, he cautioned himself not to jump to conclusions. Noelle had noticed his distraction, but Beanie decided not to burden her with his worry. Although, as his wife, Noelle was the one person he could count on to share any heavy emotional loads. But Noelle would discern his fears. And Beanie wasn't quite ready to face what he was afraid of—that Robyn was somehow involved in Henry's murder. He'd convinced himself that it was impossible. His sister was not a killer. But he didn't like having to convince himself, as though he had doubts about Robyn. Which he didn't.

Or, at least, he didn't want to have doubts.

Robyn took a sip of her latte.

Focusing on his sister, Beanie took a deep breath, inhaling the strong, aromatic smell of beans harvested from the coffee farms on St. Felipe. "What were you arguing about?"

"Who says we were arguing?"

"On the video—"

"Is there sound on the video?"

Beanie shook his head. "No, but—"

"Then what makes you think Henry and I were arguing?"

Fighting frustration, Beanie said, "The way you and Henry are gesturing at one another suggests that the conversation was heated. Several times you try to grab his arm, but he yanks it away. Then he points a finger in your face in a somewhat threatening manner."

Robyn rolled her eyes. "Okay, fine. We argued."

"About what?"

"About Liz crashing the party," said Robyn. "I told him to take out another restraining order against her. He refused. And then …"

"And then …?" prompted Beanie.

"And then he told me he was going to go for a run," said Robyn. "And he told me to go back inside and calm down, so I did. Or, I tried to calm down."

His thoughts pivoting back to the video, Beanie asked, "After you and Henry argued, where did you go?"

"What do you mean?"

"The surveillance shows you leaving the townhouse after you and Henry argued," said Beanie. "Henry left first. And then you went back inside. But about five minutes later, you left the townhouse. Then maybe about fifteen minutes later, you returned to the townhouse. Where did you go?"

Robyn sipped coffee, then said, "I went looking for Henry. I wanted to apologize to him. Tell him I was sorry about the argument. But I couldn't find him, so I went back to the townhouse and went to bed."

Nodding, Beanie tried to think if he had any other questions about the video.

Robyn said, "How did you see this video?"

"Detective Allen Green showed it to me," said Beanie. "He wanted me to see it because …"

"Because … what?" asked Robyn. "The cops think the video makes me look suspicious?"

"Janvier is suspicious," said Beanie. "Detective Green is not, but he wanted to know if you'd told me anything about where you went when you were gone from the townhouse."

Lips pursed, Robyn scoffed. "You mean, he wanted to know if I left the townhouse and followed Henry to shoot him dead and then returned to crawl into bed?"

Robyn … shot me. Beanie pushed the disturbing, intrusive thoughts away. "Janvier may be thinking along those lines, but not Detective Green."

"What does he think?" asked Robyn, removing her cell phone from her purse.

"He thinks the PC-5 killed Henry," said Beanie. "He's afraid Janvier is going to view the surveillance video as a smoking gun, go after you, and let the real killer get away."

"Detective Green is probably right," said Robyn, swiping her phone screen. "Henry was mixed up with the cartel. They probably killed him. There could be evidence against the PC-5 on Henry's laptop. That might be why the gang killed him."

"I don't know about that," said Beanie, leaning back in his chair. "If the cartel wanted Henry dead, it would have been a clean kill. Henry wouldn't have been staggering in the middle of the road. Whoever killed Henry wasn't a good shot."

"Well, it was dark," said Robyn. "Maybe the assassin had a hard time seeing Henry."

"The assassin would have had some type of infrared night scope," said Beanie.

"How do you know that?" demanded Robyn. "Oh, wait. Let me guess. Your ex-gangbanger wife explained how the PC-5 kills people, which she would know because her father—"

"Okay, what about this," interrupted Beanie, not in the mood to listen to his sister throwing shade at his wife. "If the PC-5 killed Henry because he had some evidence against them on his laptop, then why did Liz Adams steal it?"

"Maybe she didn't," said Robyn. "We don't know for sure that she did. Hey, listen, I need to go. I have a lecture I can't miss. Keep me posted."

"I will," promised Beanie, as Robyn stood and left the coffee shop.

Alone, Beanie contemplated the possibility that the PC-5 had murdered Henry. Robyn believed Henry had gotten on the bad side of the cartel, but Lime Shoes had told him that Henry and the gang had worked out an amicable arrangement. Was it possible that Henry had been double-crossing the cartel? Maybe.

Beanie finished his coffee. The disgraced doctor, Mimi Taylor, had been cleared by her alibi despite her strong motivation for murder. He was still suspicious of Dr. Liz Adams. His money was on Dr. Adams as the laptop thief. There was incriminating evidence on the laptop, but not against the island gang. Henry must have had evidence on Dr. Adams. Something damaging that could end her career. Maybe even put her in jail. Evidence Dr. Adams didn't want revealed. And it was possible she'd killed Henry, and stolen his laptop, to make sure her secrets stayed buried.

24

Beanie had finished his second coffee and was contemplating another cup when he received the text from Robyn.

Cops at townhouse w search warrant! Can u come please?

His heart dropped. Why would the police be at Henry's townhouse with a search warrant? What could they be looking for? Abandoning his plans to head to the breakroom, he grabbed his keys and left the office.

The drive to Adagio Bay seemed interminable. What should have taken fifteen minutes was taking a goat's age. Hampered by sluggish mid-afternoon traffic, Beanie gripped the wheel, trying to concentrate as he navigated the winding roads. Worst-case scenarios paralyzed him. Reflecting on his conversation with Detective Green, Beanie recalled Janvier's suspicions of Robyn. The bumbling detective believed Robyn was hiding something. Beanie had assumed Janvier meant Robyn was withholding information. Hadn't occurred to Beanie that Janvier thought his sister was hiding actual physical evidence. But what could his sister be hiding, if anything?

Beanie clutched the wheel and tried to keep the road. Just because the cops wanted to search Henry's townhouse didn't mean they were looking for something that would incriminate Robyn. Not that they would find anything to incriminate his sister, because they wouldn't. Because she didn't have anything to do with Henry's murder.

Robyn ... shot me.

Beanie pushed Henry's gasping last words from his mind. They didn't matter because they weren't true. Beanie would never believe that Robyn had killed Henry. The man had obviously been delusional in his last moments.

Thirty agonizing minutes later, Beanie arrived. Robyn stood in the breezeway, arms crossed, lips pursed. Glancing through the open front door, Beanie glimpsed cops swarming the townhouse. Wearing gloves and slip-on shoe coverings, they milled about, some conferring in small clusters, others rummaging among the furniture, lifting items from coffee tables and bookshelves. A few snapped photographs.

After making sure that Robyn was okay, considering the circumstances, Beanie asked, "When did the cops get here?"

"About twenty minutes before I texted you," said Robyn, pinching the bridge of her nose. "I was off today—studying for a test—and then the doorbell rings and it's the police. Detective Janvier shoves the search warrant in my face."

"Did you read it?"

Robyn nodded. "Says they can search every room in the townhouse."

"What are they looking for?" asked Beanie.

"Heck if I know," groused Robyn. "A needle in a haystack."

"The search warrant should tell you—"

"It said something about evidence related to Henry's murder," said Robyn. "Didn't mention anything specific. When I asked Janvier, he said he'd know what he was looking for when he found it."

Beanie dragged a hand along his jaw. "Maybe Janvier—"

"Mr. Bean ... Ms. Bean ..."

Caught off guard by the formality, Beanie glanced behind him, saw Detective Green, then faced him. The detective strode to them, his brows furrowed.

After quick, terse greetings, Beanie asked, "You know what Janvier is looking for?"

"Something he's not going to find," said Green, his mouth a grim line before he turned toward Robyn. "Sorry about all this, Ms. Bean. Trust me, I think this is a waste of the department's time and resources, but Janvier insisted."

Robyn said, "Because he's trying to find something that connects me to Henry's murder, right?"

"You don't know that," cautioned Beanie.

Robyn shook her head. "Why else would Janvier be searching the townhouse if he wasn't trying to find something to incriminate me?"

"I'm not really sure," said Green. "We're supposed to be working this case together, but he's made it clear that he doesn't want a partner. Let me see what I can find out."

After Green excused himself to return to the townhouse, Beanie turned to Robyn. "I think Green is right. Janvier is looking for a needle in a haystack."

Robyn frowned. "You think so?"

"You heard Green," said Beanie. "Janvier is not going to find anything, because there is nothing to find."

"I know that, but …"

"But … what?"

Beanie followed his sister's gaze to the townhouse's front door.

Detective Janvier stared in their direction while Green hurried out of the townhouse followed by a CSI team carrying two bankers' boxes.

"They found something," whispered Robyn.

Beanie struggled to keep the concern from his voice. "You don't know what they found. But Green will keep us in the loop, remember?"

"This is not good …"

"Don't jump to conclusions," Beanie said, not sure he could follow his own advice. What could be in those bankers' boxes? What could the cops have found? Could be anything. Maybe they were looking for something with Henry's DNA? Or evidence of someone who'd met Henry in the breezeway while Robyn was sleeping? Maybe the cops hadn't found anything. The boxes could be empty. Could be a detective's trick though he doubted it. Somehow, Beanie knew the detectives had found something damaging.

A smirk on his face, Janvier strode toward them.

"I have a bad feeling," said Robyn as the detective came closer.

A shock passed through Beanie. "What? Why?"

"Because I can't help thinking the worst," said Robyn.

Beanie said, "Well, don't, okay?"

Stopping a few feet in front of Robyn, Detective Janvier said, "Good day Bean twins."

"What is this about?" demanded Beanie. "Why are you searching my sister's townhouse."

"I had reason to believe that there was evidence in the townhouse which would lead to the identity of Dr. Montague's killer," said Janvier. "And I was right."

His heart pounding, Beanie asked, "What evidence did you find?"

"Evidence which proves that Robyn Bean killed Dr. Montague," said Janvier.

"You think I killed Henry?" Robyn asked, her voice rising, disbelief echoing through the breezeway.

"That's ridiculous!" said Beanie. "You can't be serious!"

"I assure you, Reporter Bean, that I am very serious as I never joke about murder," thundered Janvier. "Robyn Bean ... you are under arrest for suspicion of murder in the case of Dr. Henry Montague."

25

Beanie stared at the intricate shell centerpiece on the dining room table as Robyn paced back and forth.

Resisting the urge to vent his frustration, he took a deep breath. Beanie understood his sister's nervous energy because he shared it. He was anxious, as well. Two days had passed since she'd been arrested for the murder of Dr. Henry Montague. At the police station, she'd been booked, then further interrogated, but she refused to speak without an attorney present.

After bailing Robyn out of jail, Beanie had sensed she was too shaken up and shellshocked to talk. Instead of taking her back to the townhouse, he'd driven her to their parents' house in Old Oyster, the colloquial name for Old Oyster Farms. In the small, cozy den of the home where they'd grown up, Robyn relived the harrowing ordeal.

They'd discussed Robyn's predicament at length, in between his mother's fervent prayers, but Beanie felt Robyn was leaving out parts of the story. Each time he'd asked her explicitly about the new evidence against her, she was either vague or defensive, insisting she couldn't remember because it was too upsetting. Finally, Beanie's father gently chided him about badgering Robyn.

"She's been interrogated enough for today, don't you think?" asked his dad after the two of them had headed into the kitchen to make hot guava tea for the quartet.

"I'm not trying to interrogate her," protested Beanie, filling the tea kettle with water. "I'm just trying to find out why she was arrested."

"She was arrested because they think she killed Henry." His dad took four mugs from an overhead cabinet and arranged them in a line on the counter. "Which is foolish and impossible. Robyn didn't kill Henry. Your sister can have a temper sometimes, but she is not a murderer."

"I agree," said Beanie. "But I want to know more about this new evidence Janvier supposedly found. What is it? How is he connecting this evidence to Robyn? What—"

"Roland, give it a rest, son, please," implored his dad. "You'll get the answers you want, but not tonight. It's not time for you to be a reporter right now. It's time for you to be a brother and support your sister."

His father had been right, so Beanie had given it a rest, as his father requested.

Later that night, at home, after the boys had been tucked away, Beanie had shared the details with Noelle. His wife agreed that demanding answers from Robyn probably hadn't been a good idea, considering what she'd gone through. However, Noelle also believed Robyn's evasiveness should be investigated. "You think she doesn't want you to know what the evidence is against her?"

Beanie had shrugged. "That's what it seemed like. But why wouldn't she want to tell us?"

Noelle said, "Maybe the evidence makes her look guilty."

"But she didn't kill Henry."

"Just like I didn't kill anyone," reminded Noelle. "But still, the cops found evidence that sure made me look like a murderer. I didn't want you to know what the cops had found. I thought for sure it would make you wonder if maybe I was guilty."

Beanie reached for his wife's hand. "No evidence could ever make me believe that you were guilty."

"Just like there's no evidence that could make you think Robyn killed Henry."

Beanie nodded, but his stomach clenched. Noelle was right. No evidence could convince him that his sister was guilty. But what about Henry's dying words? *Robyn ... shot me.* Beanie had tried to forget those fateful words. Tried to discount them. Tell himself they didn't matter, but now ... he wasn't so sure.

"What time is it?" asked Robyn.

Beanie glanced at his watch. "It's six-thirty."

"Shouldn't she be here by now?" Robyn wrung her hands as she took another turn around the dining table. "What time did she tell you she was coming over?"

"Six o'clock," said Beanie. He'd already told Robyn the time of the appointment, but he figured her nerves had made her forgetful.

This evening, they were meeting with Attorney Octavia Constant. Beanie had called Octavia, whom he considered a friendly casual acquaintance, the day after Robyn's arrest. Octavia had agreed to meet the following evening after she spoke with the police about Robyn's case.

Known island-wide as the "Better Suspect" lawyer, Octavia had made a name for herself by searching for a better suspect for the crime her client was charged with. Octavia believed that if her client was innocent, then someone else—a better suspect—was guilty. Octavia usually got charges against her clients dropped and dismissed after finding the real perpetrator. If anyone could determine who'd killed Henry, Octavia could. Beanie had complete confidence in Octavia's ability, as the lawyer had been instrumental in getting Noelle exonerated.

Robyn glared at Beanie. "She's thirty minutes late."

Beanie sighed. "I know, but—"

"You should call her."

"I don't think—"

"Or, send her a text," Robyn demanded. "Find out what's taking her so long to—"

The doorbell rang.

Cursing under her breath, Robyn dashed out of the dining nook, across the living area, and turned the corner into the foyer. Beanie took a deep breath and tried to prepare himself for whatever Octavia had learned about Robyn's case. He worried about evidence that couldn't be explained. But things had looked bad for Noelle and she'd been vindicated. And Detective

Janvier was known for putting the cart before the horse. The man had probably jumped to the wrong conclusion.

Moments later, Octavia sat across the dining table, her expression concerned and yet confident. Beanie took a glance at Robyn. Hands clenched, his sister focused on the attorney.

Octavia said, "I won't lie to you …"

Beanie's stomach twisted.

"The evidence does look bad," said Octavia.

Robyn let out a mournful gasp. Beanie placed a hand on her back and rubbed the spot between her shoulders.

"But looks, as they say, can be deceiving," said Octavia, "and I believe they are, in your case."

"You do?" asked Robyn.

"What evidence does Janvier have?" asked Beanie.

"First of all," said Octavia, removing a file from her briefcase. "Robyn … you've hired me as your attorney and as such, our conversations are privileged and confidential. For that reason, I must ask you if you want your brother present—"

"It's okay if he's here," said Robyn, nodding. "He knows all my business and everything about me. We don't have any secrets."

Beanie nodded even though his gut clenched again. There was a secret he was keeping from Robyn. Henry's dying words. *Robyn … shot me.* But only because he wanted to protect his sister. He didn't want Robyn haunted by what had obviously been the dying man's confusion.

"Since that's settled …" Octavia opened the file. "Let's get something cleared up about the charges against you, Robyn. Janvier arrested you for suspicion of murder. In the Palmchat Islands, that's different from being arrested for murder."

Beanie nodded. "Suspicion of murder means the evidence is circumstantial?"

"And the evidence might not be strong enough to get a conviction," said Octavia. "Now, let's talk about the evidence …"

"Okay …" said Robyn.

Beanie nodded, anxious to learn why Janvier was convinced that Robyn had murdered Henry. "Detective Janvier lists the murder weapon as his main reason for arresting Robyn," said Octavia. "Her prints were on the gun."

Beanie shook his head. "That's not possible."

Octavia said, "Prints recovered from the weapon were shown to be a match for Robyn's prints which were obtained from her nursing credentials."

"I don't believe this," said Beanie, dragging a hand across his jaw. "There has to be some explanation."

"Robyn, Detective Janvier's report indicated that you couldn't explain your prints on the gun," said Octavia.

"I don't know," said Robyn, dropping her face in her hands before looking up again. "I mean … if my fingerprints are on the murder weapon … I don't know how they got there. I just know I did not shoot Henry. I didn't kill him."

"Well, that brings me to the first problematic issue," said Octavia. "The murder weapon—which had Robyn's fingerprints on it—was found in this townhouse."

Beanie asked, "Are you serious?"

"How is that possible?" asked Robyn.

"Henry was killed with his own gun," said Octavia. "The bullets recovered from Henry's body and shell casings found near the crime scene were traced to a Glock 9mm registered to Henry. So, Janvier got a warrant to search the townhouse and officers recovered Henry's gun."

"Oh my God …" wailed Robyn. "That's the gun Henry bought for protection."

"Which explains how Robyn's prints were on the gun," said Beanie.

Robyn nodded. "I fired the weapon the night Henry was killed."

Octavia gave Robyn a sharp look. "Fired it at whom?"

Beanie said, "Robyn thought someone had broken into the townhouse."

Removing a yellow legal pad and pen from her briefcase, Octavia said, "Take me through everything that happened that night. Don't leave anything out."

Beanie listened as his sister told Octavia the same story she'd relayed to him: After leaving the birthday party, she and Henry returned to the townhouse. They argued. Henry went for a run to cool down. Robyn went to bed. Around ten o'clock, she heard a noise, grabbed Henry's gun from the bedtable, then went to investigate.

"So, I fired two warning shots," said Robyn. "But I didn't hit anyone because no one broke into the townhouse. I was mistaken."

Octavia said, "Okay, that does explain your fingerprints on the gun. Tell me this—did you tell Janvier about the argument with Henry."

Robyn shook her head. "I know I should have, but ..."

"But she didn't want to give Janvier a reason to jump to the wrong conclusion," said Beanie.

Octavia said, "What did you and Henry argue about?"

After a deep breath, Robyn said, "Dr. Liz Adams."

"Who is Dr. Liz Adams?"

"She's the reason why Henry bought the gun," said Beanie.

Robyn said, "Liz was Henry's crazy ex."

"Crazy?" Octavia's right eyebrow shot up.

Robyn said, "She crashed our thirtieth birthday party. She was drunk and obnoxious."

"Spurned lover?" asked Octavia.

"Or maybe cold-blooded killer," said Beanie, eager to brainstorm "better suspects."

"She have a motive?" Octavia asked.

"Henry dumped her," said Robyn. "She was upset."

"Woman scorned," said Beanie, though he was no longer so sure that Dr. Adams had been scorned by Henry. According to the obstetrician, she and Henry had maintained their relationship while Henry was seeing Robyn. If true, the revelation was worrisome for several reasons. For one, Beanie didn't like the idea of Henry making a fool of his sister. Worse, a secret doctors with benefits situation between Henry and Liz might be misconstrued as a motive for Robyn to murder Henry.

"She tried to kill Henry," said Robyn. "He took out a restraining order against her."

"In other words," said Octavia, scribbling across her legal pad. "Dr. Liz Adams is a better suspect."

"Exactly," agreed Beanie. "Robyn told Janvier about Liz Adams, but I doubt he investigated her."

"Well, I'll have my cousin Icarus look into Dr. Adams," said Octavia.

Beanie said, "We thought another doctor—Emily Taylor—might be a better suspect, but she has an alibi."

"Why did you think she could be a better suspect?" asked Octavia.

"Henry was blackmailing her," said Robyn.

"And she might not have been the only person Henry was blackmailing," said Beanie. "Robyn saw a guy giving Henry money."

"Tell me about that," requested Octavia.

After Robyn detailed the story of Henry's meeting with the mystery man at the Fish Eyed Fool bar, Octavia said, "I'll have Icarus check out what might have been going on with that situation. Anyone else I should add to the list?"

Beanie said, "Actually, yes, but we don't know who the suspect is. We just know the identity of this suspect is in a file on Henry's laptop."

Octavia's eyes widened. "How do you know this?"

Robyn said, "Henry left me a letter that said his laptop should be given to the PIIBs because it would tell them who'd killed him."

"Did you give the laptop to the feds?" asked Octavia, writing more notes.

"I was going to, but ..."

Octavia's pen stopped, and she glanced up. "But?"

"The laptop was stolen," said Beanie. "It was supposed to be in Henry's things from his office at the hospital, but it wasn't in any of the boxes Robyn received."

"Did you alert the hospital?" asked Octavia. "Did you make them aware of the theft?"

Robyn shook her head. "I didn't think I could prove the laptop had been stolen. Or, if it even had been stolen. The orderlies who'd packed Henry's things didn't keep an inventory."

Octavia tapped her pen against the pad. "Any idea who took it?"

"My money is on Dr. Liz Adams," said Beanie. "I think the evidence on the laptop identifies her as Henry's killer."

"If that's true," said Octavia, putting her pen down and steepling her fingers. "Then we need to get that laptop."

26

"The problem is that Robyn's fingerprints are on the murder weapon," said Beanie, pacing from the dresser to the wardrobe and then back again. Much like his sister before the meeting with Octavia, Beanie had been crisscrossing the master bedroom since he and Noelle had tucked the boys beneath their covers and retired for the night.

"But that can be explained," said Noelle. "Robyn fired the gun when she thought someone had broken into the townhouse."

"I'm more worried about the surveillance video," said Beanie. "Robyn and Henry argue. Henry leaves. Robyn follows him. She says she was looking for Henry. She can't find him, so she returns to the townhouse. He doesn't. And then Robyn hears a noise and shoots two bullets at some shadows she thought might have been an intruder."

"From what you told me," said Noelle. "Janvier believes Robyn killed Henry because her prints are on the gun that killed him. Is he really concerned about the video?"

"I'm sure Janvier is convinced that Robyn left the townhouse to shoot Henry," said Beanie.

Noelle asked, "What would she have shot him with? Robyn didn't have a gun when she left the townhouse to find Henry."

"No, she didn't, but …" Beanie trailed off, recalling the conversation with his sister after Octavia left the townhouse.

"The evidence against me is pretty bad," said Robyn. "Makes me look guilty."

Beanie shrugged off her opinion. "Not necessarily."

Arms crossed, Robyn gave him a shrewd look. "Be straight with me, little brother. You're wondering if I really did kill Henry, aren't you?"

Beanie balked at her accusation, which bothered him because it was true. But his sister had seen through his pretense. As she always did.

"I don't blame you," she'd said. "I'd probably suspect me, too."

"But, I don't," said Beanie. "I know you couldn't have killed him."

"Even though my prints are on the murder weapon?" challenged Robyn.

Beanie hated the panic he'd seen in his sister's gaze. It was as though Robyn hoped he believed her but wasn't sure. Her uncertainty nearly broke his heart. He never wanted his sister to doubt his loyalty.

"Even though," he'd said, hugging her. "No matter what …"

Noelle said, "Roland?"

Beanie focused on his wife.

"Do you think Robyn shot Henry?" asked Noelle, staring at him. "Because that's crazy. Your sister didn't kill Henry."

"I know that." Beanie walked to the settee at the foot of the bed. "What I don't know is … who did?"

"Did you, Robyn, and Octavia figure out any better suspects?" asked Noelle.

"We told Octavia to check out Dr. Liz Adams," said Beanie. "And we told her about Henry's connection to the PC-5. Robyn thinks the gang could have killed him. And Detective Green agrees. But Lime Shoes said the arrangement between Henry and the mob was amicable."

"You think it wasn't?" asked Noelle. "You think Henry wanted out of the deal?"

"If that was the case," said Beanie, joining his wife in bed. "Then maybe we should take a closer look at the cartel."

Noelle said, "I would agree but …"

"But the cartel would have executed a clean kill," said Beanie.

"If Henry wanted out of the deal," said Noelle, "the PC-5 would have disappeared him. That's how they deal with guys like him. They don't leave behind bodies and shell casings to be investigated. They don't leave obvious trails for the cops to follow back to them."

As his wife snuggled next to him, Beanie let out a long exhale.

"Roland?" queried Noelle. "Why the heavy sigh?"

"What? Oh. No reason." Beanie put an arm around Noelle as he leaned back against pillows propped on the headboard. "Just worried about Robyn."

"I know the evidence looks bad, but—"

"It's not just the evidence," said Beanie, removing his arm. Sitting forward, he breathed deep, trying to calm his racing heart.

Noelle sat up. "What do you mean?"

The memory of Henry's last moments bore down upon him, a crushing weight he suddenly felt he could no longer bear. "There's something I haven't told you … "

"What haven't you told me?"

Beanie heard the sharp censure in his wife's tone. Secrets had almost torn their marriage apart. Beanie had promised to never hide things from his wife, as she'd done several years ago. But he hadn't kept that vow.

"Something I should have told the police."

"Roland, you're scaring me," said Noelle, grabbing his jaw, forcing him to look at her. "Tell me now."

After a slight hesitation, Beanie said, "You remember when Detective Green asked me if Henry was still alive when I found him?"

"And you said barely."

Beanie nodded. "Then Detective Green asked me if Henry had said anything to me."

"And you said he was moaning …"

"That wasn't exactly true," said Beanie, shoulders slumped. "Henry did say something before he died."

Gaping at him, Noelle asked, "What did he say?"

"He said …" Beanie shook his head. "Henry said … Robyn shot me …"

27

"Henry might not have been delusional..."

Beanie gaped at his sister. His thoughts scattered, he struggled to process the implication of her statement. Swallowing the lump in his throat, he stared at the mug of coffee she'd made him. He'd arrived at her townhouse around eight in the morning, after sending her a pre-dawn text, telling her he needed to see her. It was important. Imperative.

Clearing his throat, Beanie asked, "What do you mean? I don't understand..."

Robyn sighed, then ran a hand through her long, curly hair. "I mean, there might be a reason why Henry told you that I'd shot him."

"What reason could there be?" asked Beanie, though he didn't want to know the reason. Because he knew the reason. Because there was only one reason. If Henry hadn't been delusional, then...

"You weren't the only one keeping secrets," said Robyn. "There's something I need to tell you, too. Something I should have already told you. Something I should have admitted to the cops and Octavia."

His heart thudding wildly, Beanie waited, trying to prepare himself for the worst.

"I need to tell you exactly what happened the night Henry was killed," said Robyn. "From the beginning."

Trying to remain calm as his pulse raced, Beanie remained quiet as his sister spoke.

"After Henry and I left the birthday party," said Robyn. "We argued the entire drive back to the townhouse. About Liz Adams. And we kept arguing."

"Because you wanted Henry to get another restraining order," said Beanie, "but he refused to do that."

Robyn shook her head. "We argued about Liz because I'd recently found out that Henry was still sleeping with her."

Though he wasn't surprised, since Liz Adams had insinuated that she and Henry were still hooking up, Beanie was nevertheless livid. "That son of a—"

"I wanted Henry to stop hooking up with Liz," said Robyn. "But, he told me he didn't want to do that. He said he didn't want to be with me. He wanted to give the relationship with Liz another chance."

Beanie was shocked. "He wanted to be with the psycho? A woman who tried to kill him?"

"He lied about that," said Robyn. "Liz was clingy and didn't want to break up with him, but she never tried to kill him. Henry admitted to me—that's what we argued about in the breezeway—that he'd lied. There was never a restraining order."

"Why did he lie?"

Exhaling, Robyn stared at the ceiling. "I have no idea. Obviously, I knew nothing about this man. He was cheating on me. He made a deal with the PC-5, but he knew someone wanted him dead. He was blackmailing Mimi. And doing something shady with that guy in the hoodie he met at the Fish Eyed Fool."

Beanie asked, "What happened after he left to go on his run?"

"Before Henry left, he dumped me," said Robyn. "He said I could stay at the townhouse. We'd go back to being roommates, but we'd end our romantic relationship. At that point, I lost it."

"You lost it?"

"You know I'd drank too much," said Robyn. "And I was so angry and hurt and humiliated because I actually forgave Henry. I told him I was willing to start over and forget about his cheating and he still kicked me to the curb."

Beanie was upset for his sister, even though he wasn't sorry to hear that she and Henry had broken up the night of their thirtieth birthday party.

"So, I went into the house, and I got his gun," said Robyn. "The Glock he told me he'd bought to protect himself from Liz Adams. And I put it in my purse and went after Henry."

Beanie's heart sank. "You … went after Henry?"

Nodding, Robyn said, "I told you I couldn't find him, but that wasn't true. I did catch up with him. We argued some more, and he called me some insulting names and told me I needed to deal with the fact that our relationship was over. And he turned his back on me."

"And what did you do?"

Robyn sighed. "I shot at him."

At a loss for words, Beanie stared at his sister.

"But I didn't shoot him," said Robyn. "I didn't really aim at him. I wanted to scare him. And then he turned around and called me crazy, so I fired another shot. And then Henry turned and took off running."

"Did you follow him?"

"No, I went back to the townhouse," said Robyn. "I put the gun back in the drawer and I took a shower. Then I went to bed. As I was falling asleep, I heard a noise in the living room. I thought it was Henry, so I called out to him, but he didn't answer. Instead, I heard another noise. I got worried, so I grabbed the gun and went into the living room. I called out that I had a weapon. It was dark. I couldn't see well, but I thought I saw the shadow of a person slipping out of the patio doors."

"And you fired two shots?"

Robyn shook her head. "Well, yes, I did fire two shots. Two at the shadow and two at Henry when I got so mad and tried to scare him. Sorry I lied about that. Guess I need to come clean to Octavia. Hopefully, she doesn't drop me as a client."

"I don't think she will," said Beanie. "Octavia believes you're innocent. She won't like that you weren't completely honest with her, but I think she'll understand that you were worried about Janvier jumping to the wrong conclusions."

"Speaking of Janvier," began Robyn.

"What about him?"

"You need to come clean to him."

Beanie stared at his sister. "Come clean to him about what?"

"About Henry's dying words."

"Are you serious?" Beanie shook his head. "I don't think that's a good idea. The man arrested you on suspicion of murder. If I tell him what Henry said, he'll upgrade the charges."

"Janvier doesn't need Henry's last words to convince him that I'm a killer," said Robyn.

"Then why tell him?" asked Beanie.

His sister reached across the table to grab his hand. "I know you want to protect me, but I want to protect you, too."

"Protect me from what?"

"From compromising your integrity," said Robyn. "You're not the kind of person who can keep secrets and tell blatant lies. Not sharing this information must have been hard on you."

"I did feel bad about not being honest with Green," said Beanie. "But I struggled more with what Henry said and how I would figure out why he said it."

Robyn said, "Henry said what he thought was true. And I hate that. It breaks my heart that he thought I shot him in the back, but it's my fault. I never should have shot at him in the first place. I shouldn't have gotten so angry."

Beanie squeezed Robyn's hand. "Well, no, it wasn't your finest hour, Big Sis …"

Robyn let out a small, mirthless laugh. "Tell me about it."

"I'll tell you this," said Beanie. "Whoever shot Henry must have done it right after you shot at him. Makes me wonder if the person was watching the two of you. And then when you left, and Henry ran off, the killer went after him and shot him."

28

"Reporter Bean, and mind you, I use the term *reporter* with much charity," began Detective Philippi Janvier.

Sitting on the opposite side of the cluttered desk in Janvier's office, Beanie resisted the urge to roll his eyes. When it came to Janvier, he used the title detective with just as much charity, but he couldn't antagonize the man, considering his predicament.

After he and Robyn had spilled their respective beans the previous day, Beanie placed a call to Octavia. The "better suspect" attorney agreed to facilitate a meeting with Detective Janvier so Beanie could make a statement about Henry's dying words.

"I should charge you with obstruction of justice," said the detective.

"Detective, Mr. Bean recognizes and is taking responsibility for his lack of judgment, however, at the time, he was horrified, shell-shocked, and confused after discovering Dr. Montague lying in the middle of the road."

The detective scoffed. "Reporter Bean wasn't too horrified, shell-shocked, and confused to lie to Detective Green."

Beanie said, "Detective Janvier—"

"My client is attempting to rectify his mistake," interjected Octavia, "and I would hope you could appreciate that he is doing so at the detriment of his twin sister, Robyn Bean, whom you arrested for the murder of Dr. Henry

Montague. The information Mr. Bean has provided you about Dr. Montague's final words will certainly help your case against my client."

Janvier asked, "Do you expect me to reward Reporter Bean for telling the truth? Something he should have done when he was asked, point-blank by Detective Green, if Dr. Montague had said anything before he died?"

Beanie asked, "Are you going to charge me with obstructing justice, or not?"

His narrowed eyes shrewd, the detective tapped a finger against the side of his nose as he leaned back in his chair. "As I said, I should throw you in jail, but you can count yourself lucky, Reporter Bean. I shall not charge you because your attempts to subvert justice with your lies did not work."

"I did not try to subvert—"

Octavia cleared her throat.

Beanie caught her pointed look and piped down.

"As you know, I have solid and irrefutable evidence against Robyn Bean," said Detective Janvier. "As such, I do not need the last words of a dying man to solidify my case. Your sister's fingerprints are on the murder weapon used to kill Dr. Montague. That is quite enough, in my estimation, to secure a conviction."

Minutes later, after Janvier had dismissed them from his office, Beanie followed Octavia out of the St. Killian Police Station. In the hot, mid-morning sun, Beanie shielded his eyes from the glare of harsh rays as he asked Octavia, "Was telling Janvier about Henry's last words really the right thing to do?"

Donning shades, Octavia asked, "Are you wishing you had kept your mouth shut?"

Beanie's heart thudded. "What if the prosecutor wants to use Henry's dying words against Robyn?"

"Don't worry about that," said Octavia, stopping in front of her luxury sedan. "A dying declaration is usually considered an exception to the hearsay rule, but it can be successfully challenged. Specifically, statements made *in extremis* require that the individual be conscious. I could argue that Henry wasn't conscious, as you found him in a semi-conscious state, but that doesn't matter. This case is not going to trial."

Beanie nodded, though Octavia's confidence didn't abate his fears.

After the attorney departed, Beanie strode to his SUV, parked near a line of squat Sago palms. He'd dodged a bullet with the obstruction charge, but he still wasn't breathing any sighs of relief. He feared Henry's gasping last words would come back to haunt his sister. As he used the remote to open the car door, Beanie again debated his decision to come clean to Janvier. It had been the right thing to do. Even Robyn agreed. But should he have done it? Or would it have been better to—

His cell phone rang.

Beanie answered.

"I just got off the phone with Octavia," said Robyn. "She told me about the meeting with Janvier. Thank God he didn't charge you."

"Yeah, I know, but …"

"But what?"

"Maybe I shouldn't have—"

"Roland, you had to," said Robyn. "Listen, I called to tell you about another conversation I had this morning. A call from Liz Adams."

Beanie pulled his seatbelt across his chest. "What did she want?"

"You won't believe this," said Robyn. "She agreed to give me Henry's laptop."

"What? Why?" asked Beanie. "So, wait. That means she did steal it?"

"She claims she only took it because she thought Henry had explicit videos of her on the laptop," said Robyn.

"Explicit videos?"

"Revenge porn," said Robyn. "Liz said she wanted to erase the risqué videos Henry had made of her while they were together. But, it turned out there weren't any naughty videos on the laptop. So, she figured she'd give it back to me, considering that there are files on the laptop that identify Henry's killer."

"Has Liz looked at those files?"

"I don't think so," said Robyn. "She was only interested in the videos that could have harmed her reputation. Anyway, she agreed to meet me this evening, around seven, at her clinic in Handweg. Can you go with me to meet her?"

"Seven," said Beanie, remembering he had to pick up the boys from Noelle's mom's house at six. His wife would be home by six-fifteen. He could drop the boys off at home and still have time to pick up Robyn and head to Dr. Adams' clinic in Handweg.

"I should be able to," confirmed Beanie as he started the SUV.

Robyn said, "I called Detective Green. He's going to try to meet us there. Figured we might need back-up just in case Liz is trying to pull a fast one."

"Good idea," said Beanie. "I'll be at your place at six-thirty."

29

Beanie was heading into the breakroom at the *Palmchat Gazette* offices for his final five o'clock cup of coffee when his cell phone rang.

Recognizing his sister's number on the caller-ID, Beanie walked back to his cubicle as he answered.

"Change of plans," announced Robyn.

"What do you mean?"

Robyn said, "Liz wants to meet at six. She has to fly to the Bahamas tonight for some last-minute whatever. Her plane leaves at nine and she needs to head to the airport at seven."

"That time is not good for me," said Beanie, disappointment, and apprehension snaking through him. "I have to pick up the boys from my mother-in-law's house at six."

"Okay, well … I can just meet her by myself," said Robyn.

Beanie didn't like that idea. "Is Detective Green going to be there?"

"He was out on a case when I called the station," Robyn told him. "I had to leave him a message. But I'm sure he'll be there."

"If he can," said Beanie. "You don't know how long he might have to deal with the call he's on. If it's a homicide, he might be unavailable for the rest of the night."

"Look, I can meet Liz alone—"

"I don't think you should do that," protested Beanie.

"But I want to get Henry's laptop today," said Robyn.

"Can't you get the laptop when Liz returns?" asked Beanie. "Did she tell you how long she'll be gone?"

"Liz might change her mind about giving me the laptop when she gets back from the Bahamas," said Robyn. "I don't trust her."

"I don't trust her, either," said Beanie. "That's why I don't want you to meet her alone. Let me find out if Noelle's mom can keep the boys for another hour. I'll call you right back."

As Beanie suspected, his mother-in-law, who loved spending as much time as she could with the grandsons she adored, agreed to watch them for as long as Beanie needed.

Beanie called Robyn back. "Noelle's mom can watch the boys for a few more hours."

"Instead of picking me up from the townhouse," said Robyn, "just meet me at the clinic."

"Are you sure?"

"I want to get to the clinic a few minutes before six," said Robyn. "Liz might leave five minutes early and then claim I didn't show up. Like I said, I don't trust her."

"Fine," said Beanie. "See you there."

Things weren't so fine when Beanie got on the road, however.

Traffic was a nightmare due to an accident on the coastal highway. Stuck at a standstill with dozens of other vehicles, he'd pulled out his phone to text Robyn, and discovered his phone was dead. To make matters worse, he couldn't find his portable car charger. As he removed items from his glove compartment, he realized he must have accidentally left it at the office.

By the time he reached the clinic in Handweg, it was fifteen minutes after seven. Beanie's stomach dropped as he turned into the parking lot of the commercial park where the clinic was located. The place was swarming with police cruisers and two ambulances were parked haphazardly near the clinic's plate-glass entrance.

Beanie's heart simultaneously slammed and plummeted. Concern for Robyn made his gut churn. He hadn't wanted his sister to meet with Dr. Liz Adams alone. Henry's ex had proven she was unstable, capable of doing crazy things. Robyn had voiced concern over Dr. Adams' true intentions concerning Henry's laptop. What if his sister had been right? What if Dr. Adams had lied about agreeing to give Robyn the laptop? What if the OB-GYN had planned all along to lure Robyn into a trap, and—

Beanie arrested the dire thoughts. Playing the "what if" game was counterproductive and pointless. No need to jump to unfound conclusions. No need to worry until he could figure out what happened.

Exiting his car, Beanie spotted Officer Damon Fields, a source who had become a good friend, huddled with two officers. As Beanie walked toward the affable cop, Fields noticed him and then excused himself from the officers.

"You heard about the murder over the police scanner?" asked Fields.

Beanie's throat closed. Forcing the question from his mouth, he asked, "What happened?"

"Doctor found dead in her office," said Fields. "Dr. Elizabeth Adams."

Beanie was floored. "What happened to her?"

"Not sure," said Fields. "Appears to be blunt force trauma. May have been a robbery but we're not sure because there are no signs of forced entry. Could have been a patient with a late appointment. She kept a fair amount of drugs in the place, so we can't rule out robbery, but we just don't know."

After asking Fields to keep him posted, Beanie walked back to his car, shell-shocked. Dr. Liz Adams was dead. When had she been killed? Robyn had planned to meet Dr. Adams at six. Had the doctor been killed before Robyn had shown up? No, Robyn would have called him if she'd arrived at the clinic and found Liz dead. Back in the SUV, behind the wheel, Beanie tried to gather his wild thoughts. Who could have killed Liz Adams? And why?

30

"Liz is … dead?" Robyn collapsed on the couch, shaking her head. "How? What happened?"

Beanie took a seat in the chair adjacent to the couch. "From what I was able to find out, she was beaten to death."

After leaving the women's clinic where Dr. Liz Adams had been killed, Beanie drove to Hangweg to pick up Ethan and Evan from Noelle's mom's house. Though distracted and disturbed by the obstetrician's brutal murder, he'd forced himself to shift into 'daddy mode', careful to make sure the boys didn't pick up on his anxiousness. Once home, he'd put on a cartoon for the kids and started dinner. Half an hour later, when Noelle arrived, he informed her about Liz Adams' murder. Shocked and worried, Noelle agreed that Beanie should head to Robyn's townhouse after dinner.

"Beaten to death?" Robyn stared at him. "My God. Do the police have any idea who did it?"

"Not that they told me," said Beanie. "But Fields said they weren't sure. Cops have just started the investigation."

"I can't believe this," said Robyn. "Someone killed her after I left the clinic."

"That's what I'm thinking."

"But, who did it?" Robyn exhaled. "And why?"

"Fields mentioned something about Dr. Adams having drugs in the clinic," said Beanie. "It's possible that maybe a patient entered the clinic and demanded some prescription medication."

"Opioids?"

"That would be my guess," said Beanie. "You know how addictive they can be … someone desperate for drugs might have attacked her. Then again … maybe the person who killed Henry killed Liz."

Robyn frowned. "You think so?"

Beanie said, "As I was driving over, I was thinking about the PC-5."

"You think the gang killed Liz?"

Beanie said, "If Detective Green is right and the cartel killed Henry, then maybe the PC-5 knew about Henry's laptop. Maybe the gang suspected the files had evidence against them. Maybe the gang found out, somehow, that Liz Adams had taken the laptop from Henry's things. Maybe they sent someone to the clinic to confront Liz about the laptop and when she refused to give it to them, then they killed her."

Robyn said, "If that's true, then the PC-5 will probably come after me next."

"Only if Liz Adams admitted that she gave you the laptop," said Beanie.

Robyn said, "I'm sure she did, especially if someone was attacking her."

Beanie rubbed his jaw. "Yeah, but now that I think about it … I don't know."

"What don't you know?"

Beanie said, "If the cartel found out that Liz had the laptop and had her killed because she wouldn't give it to them, then why didn't they attack you first? If they found out that Liz had taken the laptop, they could have found out that Henry intended for you to get the laptop. And yet, the PC-5 never once approached you about it."

"You think your PC-5 source would know if the gang killed Liz?"

"Question is not if Lime Shoes would know," said Beanie. "Question is, would he tell me if he knows."

"You think he would tell you if the cartel thinks there's evidence against them on Henry's laptop?"

"I could mention the laptop," said Beanie. "If he knows anything about it, he might come clean to me."

"Well, speaking of the laptop," said Robyn.

"You got it?"

Standing, Robyn strode across the living area to the kitchen, where her backpack sat on the large island. Reaching into the backpack, she pulled out the laptop and then walked back to the couch. Before taking her seat again, she handed the laptop to Beanie.

Examining the thin, sleek device, Beanie asked, "Did you take a look at any of the files?"

Robyn shook her head. "I couldn't … "

Beanie was confused. "Why not?"

"It's password-protected," said Robyn. "And I couldn't figure out the password. I tried everything I could think of … Henry's birthday, where he went to medical school, his dog's name … "

"Henry had a dog?"

"When he was a kid," said Robyn. "The dog ran away. Henry was devastated. Anyway, nothing worked, so … "

"Are you going to give the laptop to the PIIBs?" asked Beanie. "Maybe they can crack the password."

"I should," said Robyn. "That's what Henry wanted me to do, but …"

"But …?"

"But I want to see the files before I give the laptop to the feds," said Robyn. "He said the identity of his killer could be found on his computer. I want to know who killed Henry."

Beanie nodded his agreement. "I definitely think we should check out the files before handing them over to the PIIBs.

Robyn exhaled, tucking a strand of her thick coils behind her ear. "But how am I going to look at the files if I don't know the password. So maybe I should give the laptop to the police."

Beanie said, "I know someone who might be able to help."

$$31$$

The next morning, Beanie maneuvered into the tiny cubicle of Stevie Bishop, his co-worker at the *Palmchat Gazette*, and said, "Hey, I've been looking for you."

Despite his laid-back attitude, surfer attire, and occasional laziness, Stevie was a decent junior reporter with a knack for research. Though he'd been born a Bishop, one of the Palmchat Islands' most prominent and wealthy families, Stevie never acted as though he was better than his significantly less wealthy colleagues. Most importantly, Stevie had a cousin who was a hacker.

No one at the newspaper had ever met the hacker, and Stevie staunchly refused to reveal anything about his cousin. No one knew the hacker's name, age, or gender. Sophie Carter, a fellow *Palmchat Gazette* reporter, suspected that there was no "hacker cousin." Sophie was convinced that Stevie was actually his hacker cousin, but Beanie wasn't sure. And it didn't matter. As long as the hacker continued to provide assistance, Beanie didn't care who he, or she, was.

"What's going on?" asked Stevie, facing his computer.

Beanie took a seat in the chair in front of Stevie's small desk. "Have you heard from your cousin about Dr. Montague's laptop?"

Beanie had given Stevie the laptop three days ago.

"Not yet," said Stevie, glancing at Beanie. "I'll text my cousin, but I'm sure my cousin is working some magic."

Nodding, Beanie tempered his disappointment. He did not doubt that Stevie's cousin would come through, but he was anxious. The identity of Henry's killer continued to confound and worry him. The laptop files could be crucial to his sister's defense. If the electronic information was credible, then it might diminish the evidence Janvier had collected against Robyn.

"So you really think there's a file on the laptop that identifies Dr. Montague's killer?" asked Stevie.

"That's what my sister and I hope," said Beanie. "Janvier is convinced she killed Henry, but that file could force him to drop the charges."

"So, the only evidence against your sister is her fingerprints on the gun, right?" asked Stevie. "I saw the article but I just skimmed it."

ARREST MADE IN CARDIOLOGIST MURDER had been written by Caleb Olivier the day after Robyn's arrest. Though once known for his diligent, tenacious investigative journalism, Caleb's writing had diminished in quality over the past few years. His stories usually lacked basic details and had to be rewritten, but Beanie had been thankful that Caleb's article had been vague. The crusty old reporter had turned in two paragraphs, hadn't bothered to request an interview with Robyn, and had forgotten to include facts given to him by the police.

Beanie said, "There's also a very problematic surveillance video which shows Robyn and Henry fighting in the breezeway outside their townhouse. Janvier is focusing on the fingerprints on the murder weapon, which Robyn can explain. She fired the gun at ..."

"At what?"

Robyn's confession flooded Beanie's mind. *I fired those bullets at Henry when I got so mad and tried to scare him.* Unwilling to confide in Stevie, Beanie said, "A shadow."

"A shadow?"

Beanie stared at Stevie, annoyed by his co-worker's dubious expression. "She fired the gun at what she thought was an intruder, but it turned out to be a strange shadow."

Leaning back in his chair, Stevie looked toward the ceiling. "But ... I just wonder ..."

"Wonder what?" asked Beanie, mindful of his tone, considering that he needed Stevie's help. Didn't need to irritate the scion.

"How was Dr. Montague killed with his own gun?" asked Stevie. "You know, if your sister used it to shoot at a shadow—"

"She did," interjected Beanie, listening for any doubt in Stevie's voice.

"Then, after she shot at the shadow, what did she do?"

Beanie said, "She called me. Told me she thought someone had broken into the townhouse."

Stevie said, "So … both your sister and the killer used the same gun the night Dr. Montague was killed. Your sister shot at a shadow. The killer shot Dr. Montague. Question is, who shot first?"

Beanie frowned. "What do you mean?"

"Did your sister shoot at the shadow before the killer shot Dr. Montague?" asked Stevie. "Or, did the killer shoot Dr. Montague before your sister shot at the shadow?"

Beanie frowned. "You know, I don't think—"

The cell phone in the pocket of his tan chinos vibrated.

"My phone." Beanie pulled it out to answer. "Just a second. Roland Bean …"

"Octavia just called," said Robyn, her tone rushed, breathless.

Beanie's stomach clenched. "What's happened?"

"Detective Janvier wants to question me again," Robyn said. "Can you meet us at the police station?"

32

"I know exactly what Janvier is going to ask you, Robyn," said Octavia, sitting in the chair directly across from Beanie and Robyn.

An hour had passed since Robyn's breathless phone call, telling Beanie that Detective Janvier had requested a second interrogation. After leaving the *Palmchat Gazette*, Beanie arrived at the St. Killian police station in fifteen minutes. Octavia and Robyn had been in the waiting room, a spacious area painted powder blue, with wide windows and rows of vinyl-covered chairs.

Beanie's gut twisted.

The anxiousness he'd managed to ignore as he'd driven to the police station returned. Navigating the traffic through downtown St. Killian, Beanie had a feeling that Janvier was about to surprise his sister with more incriminating evidence. Beanie didn't think he could deal with more clues that incriminated his sister. He knew she hadn't killed Henry, but he'd be lying to himself if he didn't admit to experiencing moments of doubt. At times, he had to convince himself not to think the worst.

The worst being that Robyn really had killed Henry.

Instead of jumping to conclusions, Beanie focused on the conversation he'd been having with Stevie Bishop before Robyn called.

Stevie's question intrigued him. Beanie hadn't thought much about the timeline of the events that had occurred the night Henry was killed. Now he wondered, how had Henry's killer gotten the gun? Beanie recalled the series of events concerning the gun, according to Robyn.

His sister had argued with Henry before he left to go for a late evening run on the beach. During the argument, Henry had dumped Robyn. Angry, hurt, and humiliated, Robyn went into the townhouse and got the firearm Henry had purchased for protection. After following Henry to the dunes, Robyn argued again with Henry. The cardiologist had given her the harsh truth, then turned away, dismissing her. Enraged, Robyn fired two shots, hoping to frighten him. Returning to the townhouse, she'd taken a shower and then gone to bed. Awakened by a strange noise, she'd taken the gun from the bedtable drawer. In the dark living room, she saw a shadow and fired two shots, realizing it was just a shadow.

As Beanie circled the police station visitor's lot, he concluded that the killer couldn't have stolen Henry's gun *after* Robyn shot at the shadow. The more Beanie thought about it, the more he realized that Henry's killer had to have removed the gun from the bedtable *before* Robyn shot at the shadow.

Pulling into an empty parking space, Beanie decided that the only thing which made sense was also more than a little unbelievable. Robyn returned to the townhouse with the gun after shooting at Henry. She returned the gun to the bedtable drawer. The killer had to have broken into the townhouse, taken the gun, gone after Henry, shot him, and then returned the gun to the bedtable. Robyn, tired and hungover, hadn't heard anything. Until she heard what she'd initially thought was an intruder.

There were issues with the theory, Beanie knew. Things that didn't make sense. Lots of unanswered questions. Could the killer really have broken into the townhouse twice without Robyn realizing it? Had his sister been that hungover? And how would the killer have known where to find the gun?

Beanie struggled with the holes in the theory, but they would have to wait.

Focusing on Octavia, he resolved to give the attorney his complete attention.

"Detective Janvier wants to question Robyn about the murder of Dr. Elizabeth Adams," said Octavia.

"What?" Robyn shook her head.

A jolt passed through Beanie. "Why?"

Octavia angled toward Robyn. "Did you meet with Dr. Adams the day she was killed?"

Robyn nodded. "I went to her clinic around six that day."

"Why?" asked Octavia.

"Remember the laptop that belonged to Henry," said Robyn.

"We told you we thought Dr. Adams had stolen it," reminded Beanie.

"I went to get the laptop from Liz," said Robyn. "She'd agreed to give it to me because I told her the laptop had files that would identify Henry's killer."

Octavia said, "And you got the laptop from Dr. Adams?"

Robyn nodded. "I tried to look at the files, but the laptop was password-protected, and I have no idea what the password is."

"I told her to give it to me," said Beanie. "I know a guy who knows a guy who might be able to figure out the password."

Octavia held up a hand. "Say no more, please. I don't need to know how you get the information. I only need to know the contents of the files."

Beanie nodded. "I'll let you know as soon as I find out."

"There's something I need to tell you," began Robyn.

His stomach clenching again, Beanie waited, fearful of what his sister would disclose.

"Please do," encouraged Octavia. "I don't like surprises."

After a quick exhale, Robyn said, "Before Liz agreed to give me the laptop, we did exchange a few heated text messages. Janvier might know about them."

"I'm sure he requested Dr. Adams' phone records," agreed Octavia. "How heated were these messages?"

"Did you threaten to kill Dr. Adams?" blurted Beanie.

Robyn glared at him before rolling her eyes. "Of course, I didn't. But I did tell her that if she didn't give me the laptop, I was going to make her give it to me …"

Shaking his head, Beanie cursed. "You never should have gone to meet her without me. You wouldn't be in this mess if—"

"Well, I did," Robyn shot back. "And I am in this mess, so—"

"This is counterproductive," interjected Octavia. "We don't have time for shoulda, woulda, coulda, okay? Now, the texts could be a problem because I am sure Janvier will decide to misconstrue them but making someone hand over a laptop is not the same as knocking them over the head."

Beanie frowned. "What?"

Octavia said, "Dr. Adams was beaten to death with a paperweight on her desk. It was square, with very sharp edges, and featured a 3-D Caduceus symbol displayed in the middle."

Beanie frowned. "A Caduceus?"

Robyn said, "It's the medical symbol. You know, the snake wrapped around the pole. I remember that paperweight."

Glancing at his sister, Beanie asked, "You do?"

"I noticed it because Henry had a paperweight just like it," said Robyn. "I questioned Liz about it. Accused her of taking it, actually. She claimed she and Henry received the same paperweight from an administrator at a hospital in St. Basil where they'd both worked."

Octavia asked, "Did you touch the paperweight?"

Beanie's heart kicked. "Why would you ask her that?"

"Because Robyn's fingerprints are on that paperweight," said Octavia.

"What?" Beanie asked. "How?"

Nodding, Robyn said, "Because I picked up the paperweight … and then I saw Liz's name engraved on it, so I put it down. That's how my fingerprints got on the paperweight. I didn't pick it up to hit her with it."

"Is that what Janvier thinks?" Beanie stared at Octavia. "That Robyn killed Liz Adams?"

"That would be my guess," said Octavia.

"I didn't kill Liz," said Robyn, her voice rising in anger and protest. "She was absolutely alive when I left the clinic."

"Is there anyone who can corroborate your story?" asked Octavia. "Were there any patients at the clinic when you arrived?"

Robyn exhaled, shaking her head. "Liz had closed the clinic early. Her staff was already gone. It was just me and her."

Octavia said, "Don't worry, okay."

Beanie fought to keep his frustration. "How can she not worry? You know how Janvier gets when he's so sure that he's got the right suspect. Even if we do find evidence to exonerate Robyn, he'll ignore it."

"Maybe Janvier will ignore the truth," said Octavia. "But the prosecutor won't. My godfather is the Director of Public Prosecutions, remember? He is not in the habit of allowing his employees to engage in foolish prosecutorial shenanigans. Which is to say, his prosecutors don't take cases they know they can't win."

Slumping back in the chair, Beanie nodded.

"Speaking of Janvier," said Robyn. "Where is he?"

Octavia glanced at her watch. "Janvier was supposed to meet with us at three."

Robyn said, "He's twenty minutes late."

Octavia stood. "Let me find out what's keeping him."

33

As the attorney walked away, Robyn took out her phone and gave the device her full attention. The silent treatment, thought Beanie, not surprised by his sister's passive-aggressiveness. Well, he wasn't really in the mood to talk with her at the moment anyway. Rising from his chair, Beanie mumbled that he was going to the men's room. Robyn shrugged but said nothing.

Moments later, in the restroom, Beanie bypassed the two urinals—both occupied, one by a uniformed officer and the other by another civilian—and went into the last of the three stalls. He didn't mind. Wasn't as though he really needed to relieve himself. He'd just needed to get away for a moment. Clear his scattered thoughts.

Staring at the toilet, Beanie took a few deep breaths.

Why had Robyn gone to meet Dr. Adams without him? If she'd only waited, then—

No. Beanie shook his head. He wasn't going to play the "what if" game. He needed to focus on helping his sister clear her name.

Turning toward the stall door, Beanie heard, "… he is an absolute imbecile!"

Beanie cringed. He recognized the rude, grating French accent. Detective Philippi Janvier. Cursing under his breath, Beanie lamented his decision to visit the men's room. Why hadn't he taken a walk outside?

"Well, I don't think he did it on purpose."

The second voice was familiar, as well. Officer Damon Fields was also in the restroom. The detective and the affable cop were discussing something. No, someone. An absolute imbecile, according to Janvier. Well, he should know, figured Beanie.

"Intentional, or not, it was a stupid mistake!" thundered Janvier. "His incompetence could ruin the case against Robyn Bean."

Beanie froze. Janvier and Fields were discussing Robyn. Should he make himself known? Clear his throat? Flush the toilet? Or … stay quiet and listen? Wait to determine if Janvier would reveal something that might help Robyn's case.

"Well, I don't think—"

"I don't need you to think," said Janvier. "I just need you to make sure that no other piece of evidence is destroyed!"

Seconds later, Beanie heard the men's room door open and then close.

Curious about the conversation, he exited the stall. Officer Fields remained in the restroom, examining what looked like a razor bump under his chin. Shocked, Beanie caught the policeman's equally shocked gaze in the mirror.

"Beanie?" Fields faced him. "What are you doing in here?"

"The urinals were taken when I came in," said Beanie, crossing to the basin. He pumped foamy soap into his palm from the wall-mounted dispenser and turned on the taps. "Had to take a stall."

"Guess you heard Janvier going off?" asked Fields, soaping his hands.

Beanie nodded, working a lather between his palms. "What was that about? Who's the imbecile?"

Fields scoffed. "The imbecile is Janvier."

Beanie chuckled as he thrust his hands under the stream of warm water.

Fields finished his hands and stepped to the paper towel dispenser. "He's mad at Green."

"Detective Green?" Beanie frowned at the soapy water circling the drain. "What did he do?"

Drying his hands, Fields said, "Detective Green obtained exterior video surveillance from outside Dr. Liz Adam's clinic the day she was killed."

"Why is Janvier upset about that?"

"Because Green accidentally erased it," said Fields. "But Janvier suspects Green did it on purpose."

"Why would Green purposely erase surveillance video?" asked Beanie, wondering if the video might have shown his sister leaving the clinic before Dr. Adams had been killed.

Fields tossed the crumbled towel in the trash can. "Janvier thinks Green likes your sister."

"What?" Beanie turned off the faucet and grabbed a towel to dry his hands.

"I know, it's crazy," said Fields. "I mean, it's not crazy that Green might be interested in your sister. She's a good-looking woman, but he's not going to compromise the case. Green is a good detective. He just made a mistake."

"How did Green erase the video?" questioned Beanie, throwing his used towel away.

Fields shrugged. "Claims he accidentally pushed the wrong buttons when he was trying to upload the video. The strip center owner has a pretty unsophisticated surveillance system. Some kind of closed-circuit setup that records to a DVD. Green got the DVD and was trying to upload the video to our computers. I guess he thought he'd completed the upload, but he'd actually deleted the video from the DVD."

"There's no backup DVD?"

Fields shook his head. "That's why Janvier is going ballistic. He wants Green fired."

"Fired?" Beanie shook his head. "That seems a bit extreme, don't you—"

The radio on Field's duty belt squawked.

After answering it, Fields headed toward the exit, telling Beanie, "Hey. I gotta take off. Good to see you."

"Let me know about any other developments," said Beanie.

"Will do," promised Fields.

Alone in the men's room, Beanie took a deep breath. His phone vibrated, signaling a text. He read the message. *With Octavia and Janvier now. He doesn't want you at the meeting. Will call later and let you know what happened.*

Beanie stared at his reflection in the mirror. A jolt passed through him. He worried about Janvier's questions concerning the murder of Dr. Liz

Adams. Robyn hadn't killed the OB-GYN. Still, he had a feeling the incompetent, overzealous detective would jump to the wrong conclusion and accuse his sister of murder. Again.

34

Sipping his last cup of coffee of the day, Beanie turned toward the computer on the small desk in his tiny cubicle in the *Palmchat Gazette* offices. He grabbed the mouse, made a few clicks, and opened the file of his latest article. Normally, fact-checking details before he sent the final draft to Vivian for additional edits and comments, was a chore. Today, Beanie didn't mind. The past few days had been slow, but he was glad for the opportunity to think about Robyn's case.

Beanie still felt a painful jolt when he thought about the murder charges his sister faced.

The jolt was even more painful when he considered the most recent accusations against Robyn. The meeting with Janvier had progressed as Beanie expected. The detective believed that the same person who'd killed Henry had killed Dr. Liz Adams. And that same person was Robyn.

The evidence was circumstantial, but Janvier was convinced Robyn had beaten Liz to death with a paperweight. Beanie conceded that events leading to Liz's murder might make his sister look suspicious. Robyn had met Liz at the woman's clinic during a time when there were no patients or staff. Before the meeting, Robyn exchanged contentious text messages with Liz. Robyn didn't have an alibi for the time of Liz's murder. And, once again, his sister's fingerprints were on the murder weapon.

But none of the evidence proved that Robyn had killed Dr. Liz Adams.

Exhaling, Beanie tried to focus on the article. After Janvier's interrogation, Beanie, his sister, and Octavia discussed strategy and potential better suspects over coffee at a Hullabaloo coffee shop near the police station.

Later that night, after the boys had been bathed, and tucked into bed, Beanie and Noelle had discussed the disturbing developments. His wife agreed that he couldn't let Janvier railroad his sister. He needed to find a better suspect as soon as possible. After learning that Dr. Emily Taylor had an airtight alibi for the night of Henry's murder, Beanie had revised his potential better suspect list. The list had to be revised again after Liz Adams' death.

That left the PC-5.

For some reason, Beanie didn't think the cartel was behind Henry's death.

As he continued fact-checking the article, Beanie reflected on the guy in the hoodie Robyn had told him about. The mystery guy Henry had met at a seedy bar in Little Turkey. The guy had given Henry an envelope full of cash. Had the money been some sort of payoff? Blackmail money? It was possible. Henry was a confirmed extortionist. He'd blackmailed Dr. Emily Taylor. And he was in dire straits financially, as evidenced by his willingness to borrow money from the mob. Working for the cartel took care of the debt Henry owed the gang, but he was still desperate for cash.

Henry might have had damaging evidence on the mystery guy. Something that could ruin his life, or send him to jail, or maybe get the guy killed. The mystery guy might have been tired of paying Henry and decided to kill him.

Beanie sat back in his chair. There was still the question of how the mystery guy managed to shoot Henry with the gun Henry had bought for protection. The same gun Robyn had used to shoot at Henry before she'd shot at the shadows in her living room.

Beanie rubbed his chin. He supposed—

His phone beeped, signaling a text.

Reading the message, his heart slammed.

got info for you. See me when you get off work

35

"I heard that there's a detective in the St. Killian Police Department who believes the PC-5 had something do with that doctor's murder," said Lime Shoes. "You need to know that's not true. And you probably shouldn't write about that theory in the *Palmchat Gazette*."

Understanding the not-so-subtle threat, Beanie tried to temper his apprehension as his gaze dropped to the scarred, lacquered table. At thirty minutes after five o'clock, he sat across from the old PC-5 gangster in the booth near the back of the Purple Gecko, the seedy Handweg bar where Lime Shoes conducted business.

An hour ago, after receiving the text from the old gangster, Beanie had been on pins and needles, wondering what Lime Shoes wanted to discuss with him. Worrying about the conversation. Wishing Lime Shoes had given him details in the text.

Beanie had wanted to call the cartel member but knew better than to attempt to take liberties. Lime Shoes dictated the relationship, which Beanie wanted to remain on the best terms possible. So, if Lime Shoes demanded he wait, then he'd wait.

Didn't stop him from speculating, however. Or hoping Lime Shoes might confirm that the PC-5 had ordered a hit on Henry.

"But you can, and should, write about this …"

Beanie glanced up.

Lime Shoes took a sip of whiskey, then said, "There's a dirty cop working in the St. Killian Police Department," said Lime Shoes.

Beanie held himself rigid, resisting the urge to gape at the old gangster or ask him to repeat the bombshell revelation he'd just dropped. His mind blown, Beanie struggled to gather his scattered thoughts and rein in his wayward excitement.

Raising his glass of whiskey, Lime Shoes peered at the dark amber liquid. "Apparently, this bad cop likes to shake down suspects and steal valuables from crime scenes. Often, while investigating robberies, he'll snatch expensive items that weren't stolen, and then list them as property taken from the residence."

"Are you serious?" whispered Beanie, his pulse skyrocketing.

Nodding, Lime Shoes said, "He even ran a few scams with a partner. Worked this way. The partner would find victims—older, wealthy people—and the dirty cop would have one of his confidential informants break into the wealthy victim's house and steal their valuables. How I know about this is because one of my crew members used to work for the cop before he started working for me."

"So your crew member told you about the dirty cop?"

"That's not all he told me," said Lime Shoes. "He said the dirty cop's partner … was Dr. Henry Montague."

36

"A dirty cop in the St. Killian police department?" Detective Green let out a long exhale. "Well, can't say I'm surprised. I'll bet the guy is a PC-5 plant. The cartel has moles everywhere."

Taking a sip of his latte, Beanie glanced around Pourciau Square. On a sunny afternoon at four o'clock, the place bustled with tourists and residents. The detective had agreed to meet at the spot where he'd told Beanie about the surveillance video at Henry's townhouse. After grabbing a coffee from the Hullabaloo café cart, Beanie and the detective found an empty wooden bistro table. While his latte grew lukewarm, Beanie informed Green about the dirty cop, taking care not to reveal his source.

Following the bombshell information about Henry working with a dirty cop in the St. Killian police department, Beanie had driven home in a daze. Though shocked and dismayed, he nevertheless managed to take care of both "daddy" and "husband" duties without betraying his distraction.

This morning at work, Henry's scams with the dirty cop dominated his mind, stealing his attention from all other tasks. Lime Shoes hadn't told him the identity of the dirty cop. The old gangster claimed his crew member knew the cop by a nickname.

"Called him Mag Flo," Lime Shoes had said. "Didn't know his real name."

As for what the dirty cop looked like, Lime Shoes said the crew member described him as a light-skinned West Indian.

"Half the men in the Palmchat Islands are light-skinned West Indians," Beanie had pointed out.

With an unapologetic shrug, Lime Shoes agreed, then advised Beanie to focus his efforts on identifying the dirty cop. "That's the suspect you need to look into."

"You think the dirty cop could have had something to do with Henry's murder?"

Lime Shoes had said, "I think you better find out."

The more Beanie reflected on the revelations provided by Lime Shoes, the more he was convinced that the gangster was right.

Henry's killer had been revealed—the dirty cop had murdered the cardiologist. There was no honor among thieves, as the saying went, and Beanie imagined some sort of fall out between Henry and the dirty cop. A disagreement about money. Greed was a powerful motive for murder. Lots of people had lost their lives over money. Henry could have met a likewise fate.

Beanie didn't know what to think, or how to feel. He was excited. Elated. Relieved. Finally, there was a "better suspect," someone who absolutely wanted Henry dead. Problem was, the dirty cop's identity was unknown.

Beanie said, "The PC-5 is known for directing cartel members to become cops so they can taint and destroy evidence, and keep the gang informed about operations and investigations against them. But I don't think the dirty cop is PC-5."

Green frowned. "Why not?"

Knowing he couldn't be completely honest, Beanie glanced away from Green's hard, suspicious gaze. "I told you it was an anonymous tip. Well, the person who called it in didn't mention the PC-5 and I think they would have."

"An anonymous tip means the caller could have been lying to you," said Green.

"I don't think so," said Beanie. "I think the tip was legit. Which means … this dirty cop, whoever he is, might have killed Henry Montague."

After another sip of coffee, Green exhaled. "I need to find out who this dirty cop is …"

"I agree," said Beanie. "Question is, how to find out?"

"I think the PIIB needs to get involved," said Green.

"Island feds?" asked Beanie.

"You may not think the PC-5 is involved," said Green, "but I still think the crooked cop might be on the cartel's payroll."

Remembering the conversation with Lime Shoes, Beanie said, "I suppose it's possible, but …"

Green said, "I have a PIIB contact we can talk to. You can tell him your story."

Nodding, Beanie asked, "When can we meet him?"

"What time is it?" Green raised his arm, looked at his bare wrist, then cursed under his breath. "Still need to get a new watch."

Beanie consulted his old Timex. "Ten minutes to five."

Green said, "I'll see if he can meet us in an hour, or so …"

37

"By the way, I don't think your sister killed Dr. Liz Adams," said Green, steering the sedan around a traffic circle in downtown St. Killian.

In the passenger seat, Beanie scoffed. "Tell that to Detective Janvier."

"Believe me, I tried," said Green. "He's made it clear that he doesn't need or value my opinions or theories."

"Did you tell him that you were going to the clinic to be there when Robyn met with Dr. Adams?" asked Beanie.

"I did," said Green. "But, since I wasn't able to make it, I can't prove that Robyn didn't kill Dr. Adams."

Beanie said, "I don't think it would have mattered to Janvier even if you could prove that Robyn didn't kill Liz. He's convinced that Robyn has a motive."

Three hours had passed since Beanie's conversation with Detective Green in Pourciau Square. Following Green's promise to reach out to his PIIB contact, Beanie returned to the *Palmchat Gazette* offices. He finished his fact-checking, keeping his eye on his phone, anxious for Green's call. When Green hadn't contacted him by five-thirty, Beanie fought disappointment and left the office. He was eager to talk to the PIIB agent but figured Green's contact might not have been available on such short notice. Or maybe Green had been sent out on a call.

When the detective sent him a text around eight o'clock, Beanie had just finished dinner with his family. After explaining to Noelle that he needed to meet with Detective Green about Robyn's case, Beanie drove to the St. Killian police station. He and Green headed out to meet the PIIB contact in Green's police-issued vehicle.

"Janvier mentioned the laptop Robyn claimed Dr. Adams had stolen from Dr. Montague's office at St. Killian General." Green left the traffic circle and veered onto the coastal highway that circled the island. "I told him that Robyn said Dr. Adams planned to give her the laptop."

"I'm guessing he didn't believe you," said Beanie.

"I told Janvier that Dr. Adams had more of a motive to kill Robyn than the other way around," said Green. "Robyn told me the laptop has a file that identifies Henry's killer. Maybe Dr. Adams stole it because the file shows she killed Henry."

"Initially, that's what Robyn and I thought," said Beanie. "But when Liz Adams gave Robyn the laptop, she admitted that she was looking for files Henry had made of the two of them in an intimate setting. When she realized the laptop didn't have any files that would embarrass or humiliate her, she was willing to hand it over."

"Which means your sister had no reason to kill Dr. Adams," said Green.

Nodding, Beanie said, "Someone did. But who? And why?"

Green said, "Maybe, Dr. Adams discovered that the files identified the mole working in the police department. She might have given the laptop to Robyn so the dirty cop wouldn't target her, but he killed her anyway."

Beanie sighed. "And now Robyn has the laptop. What if the dirty cop comes after my sister?"

"Maybe Robyn should give the laptop to the police," suggested Green.

"That's what Henry wanted her to do," said Beanie. "But, honestly, Robyn and I wanted to check out the files before we turned them over to Janvier. We were worried he might destroy them, especially if they don't support his theory that Robyn killed Henry."

The detective used his indicator to change lanes. "Who did the files identify as Henry's killer?"

"We don't know," admitted Beanie. "The laptop is passport protected."

"The department may be able to figure out the password," said Green.

Beanie said, "I already gave it to a friend to help figure out the password. My co-worker Stevie Bishop has a cousin who's a hacker. If he's able to get into the laptop, we'll let you know."

"What's the hacker's name?" asked Green.

Exhaling, Beanie said, "I wish I knew. Stevie won't reveal his identity."

Green said, "I was asking because I wondered if the hacker could recover lost video."

Though he recalled Officer Fields telling him about Green's gaff with the surveillance video, Beanie decided to keep the information to himself. He didn't want to betray Fields' confidence or embarrass Detective Green. He'd wanted to ask the detective about the video but didn't know how to bring up the subject. Now that he knew about the PC-5 mole, however, he was more interested in investigating Henry's laptop than examining more surveillance video.

"He might be able to recover video," said Beanie. "Why do you ask?"

"Janvier's upset with me because I accidentally erased surveillance video from the cameras outside Dr. Adams' clinic," said Green. "He thinks I destroyed the video on purpose."

"Why would he think that?" asked Beanie, though Fields had already told him.

"He thinks I'm in love with your sister," said Green. "And I'm hoping to win her heart by getting rid of evidence that would prove she murdered Dr. Montague."

Beanie asked, "Is that true?"

Green scoffed as he turned from the main road onto a side street. "Of course not. It's ridiculous and insulting. I mean, don't get me wrong. Your sister is pretty and she seems nice, but I hardly know her. How could I be in love with her? And I would never deliberately compromise an investigation."

"I didn't think you would," said Beanie, glancing through the passenger window at the familiar surroundings of Little Turkey. The lower-middle-class neighborhood was home to the island's industrial sector, with factories and warehouses clustered among the enclaves of modest homes. The area enjoyed decent employment, what with its proximity to the airport, where most residents worked, but there was plenty of disenfranchisement and disenchantment to complain about. Little Turkey residents were vocal about civil rights and often staged protests to demand basic services.

Moments later, when Green turned into the parking lot of a bar called The Fish Eyed Fool, Beanie chuckled his surprise.

"Something funny?" asked Green.

Beanie shook his head. "Just the name of this place."

Like most seedy drinking establishments in Little Turkey, the Fish Eyed Fool looked dilapidated and downtrodden in the fading sunlight. Constructed of driftwood and corrugated siding, the main structure, which had probably once been a fruit stand, was surrounded by cheap plastic tables. Several customers milled around the bar, talking, and laughing. A few couples sat at tables, enjoying a late evening libation.

Driving around potholes, the detective found a parking space beneath a tall palm tree.

Moments later, sitting at one of the dusty plastic tables, Green said, "I'm more upset with myself about the video I accidentally erased than Janvier could ever be."

"Why's that?" asked Beanie, frowning as he stared at the film of fine dust on the glasses of water the waitress had brought them minutes ago.

Leaning over the table, Green said, "I took a look at it before I ruined it. The video shows several exterior angles of the women's clinic. One of the images is Robyn leaving the clinic. Ten minutes later, a man shows up and enters the clinic."

Beanie asked, "You think he killed Dr. Adams?"

"I don't think he walked into the clinic and found the doctor dead," said the detective. "I think Liz Adams was alive when the man entered. And when he exited, he seemed to be in a hurry, and he was glancing around. He walked quickly across the street and out of view of the cameras. I estimate he was in the clinic for fifteen, maybe twenty minutes."

"Enough time to kill her," said Beanie.

Green nodded. "I was hoping to get a still shot of the guy, have the photo enlarged and enhanced, and then run through the island criminal database index."

"Maybe you can still do that," said Beanie. "Maybe have a sketch artist do a rendering."

"Not sure it'll do any good."

"Why do you say that?"

"Guy was wearing a hoodie, baseball cap, and sunglasses," said Green. "I got a good look at him, but I don't really know what he looks like."

A jolt passed through Beanie. "A guy in a hoodie and sunglasses?"

Green nodded.

Beanie said, "I know him."

"You do?"

"Well, I don't *know* him, that is, I don't know his name or who he is," clarified Beanie. "But, I think he was involved in something shady with Henry Montague."

Frowning, Green asked, "Something shady?"

"Robyn saw him a few times meeting with Henry," Beanie said, then went on to tell Green about the guy in the hoodie who'd given Henry the envelope of cash.

"Actually, Henry and the guy meet here at this bar," said Beanie. "The Fish Eyed Fool."

"Did Robyn get a good look at the guy?"

"She couldn't see what he looked like," said Beanie. "She was watching from her car. She didn't want Henry to catch her spying so she was too far away to discern his features or anything distinguishing about him."

Green rubbed his jaw. "Well, that's interesting. The same guy who may have had something to do with the murder of Dr. Adams could also be the same man who might have been working a scam with Dr. Montague. Which could mean …"

"What?" prompted Beanie.

"What if the guy in the hoodie killed Henry," suggested Green.

Beanie shook his head. "I think the dirty cop killed Henry. They were running a scam."

"Henry seems to have been running scams with and blackmailing everybody on this island," said Green. "Sure, he was working with the dirty cop, but he could have had another scheme going with the guy in the hoodie. If they argued about money, the guy in the hoodie could have killed Dr. Montague. And Dr. Adams, too."

"Maybe because Dr. Adams knew that the guy in the hoodie killed Henry?" asked Beanie, warming to the theory.

"It's possible," said Green, leaning back in his chair. "Maybe Dr. Adams was in on the scam between Dr. Montague and the hoodie dude."

Beanie shook his head. "I don't think—"

"Hold on a sec …" Green held up a finger, then reached inside his jacket and pulled out his phone.

Beanie exhaled. Staring at the sticky surface of the dingy plastic table, he thought about the guy in the hoodie. He was willing to concede that maybe the guy had killed Henry, but—

Green cursed.

Glancing up, Beanie asked, "What is it?"

"My PIIB contact can't make it," said Green. "Got called to interview a new witness on a case he's handling."

Beanie hid his disappointment. "Maybe he can meet us another day?"

Green said, "I'll try to set it up. In the meantime, I'll try to figure out if the dirty cop really exists and, if so, who he is. Why don't you ask your co-worker about his hacker friend."

Beanie nodded. "Hopefully, he can recover the video. It would be good to have proof that my sister *wasn't* the last person to see Dr. Adams alive."

38

"There's a dirty cop in the St. Killian police department," echoed Sophie Carter, eyes wide, jaw dropped.

"Is that right?" asked Caleb Olivier, eyes narrowed, his penetrating glare suspicious. "And who told you that?"Beanie squirmed in his chair, regret snaking through him. Maybe he shouldn't have told his co-workers about the mystery mole. Lime Shoes hadn't specifically requested that he keep the knowledge to himself, and Beanie had already decided to inform Robyn and Octavia Constant. The conversation with his sister and her attorney had been intense, hopeful, and cautious. On the one hand, they were optimistic about the idea of a viable "better suspect." On the other, they acknowledged that uncovering the bad cop would be a daunting task.

Sitting on the edge of Beanie's small desk, Sophie rolled her eyes. "Were you not listening, Caleb? Did you not hear, or maybe understand, when Beanie said one of his informants told him?"

"I not only heard, young lady, but I completely and thoroughly understood," said Caleb, standing near the entrance of Beanie's cubicle. "Do not question my hearing or my mental capacity."

"Sorry, Caleb," said Sophie, her tone not entirely contrite. "I wasn't trying to imply that you can't hear or comprehend. I was just reminding you that Beanie already told us who told him about the mole."

"I didn't need to be reminded," admonished Caleb. "There is nothing wrong with my memory, either. I asked that question because I'm a reporter. It's my job to get to the bottom of things and I am nowhere near the bottom of this situation."

Beanie sighed. "My source prefers to remain anonymous."

"And you have no idea who the dirty cop is?" asked Caleb.

Trying to ignore the old man's blatant skepticism, Beanie said, "None whatsoever. But I've informed Detective Green. He's got a contact in the PIIB—"

"What did Green's contact say?" asked Sophie.

"We didn't get a chance to talk to him," said Beanie. "The contact was called away on another case. Reminds me that I need to call Green and ask if he's rescheduled the meeting. In the meantime, Green is going to try to figure out who the bad cop might be."

Harrumphing, Caleb said, "That's the least he could do, considering that he ruined good evidence."

"He didn't mean to do that," said Beanie, regretting telling Caleb and Sophie about the video surveillance Green had accidentally erased.

"Intentional, or not," began Sophie, arms crossed, "that video could have helped Robyn's case."

Nodding, Caleb said, "The video from the clinic could have proved that she didn't kill Dr. Adams."

"Yeah, I know," said Beanie, trying to temper his disappointment. Robyn and Octavia had expressed the same sentiments. Octavia, especially, believed that Green's mistake was an egregious error akin to obstruction of justice.

Sophie said, "So let's hope he can redeem himself by finding the dirty cop."

"If there is a dirty cop," said Caleb.

"There is a dirty cop," said Beanie. "And he might have killed Henry. He passes the motive, means, and opportunity test. The bad cop and Henry ran a scam together and it's possible they had a disagreement, possibly about money, and the bad cop decided to get rid of Henry."

"Makes sense," said Caleb, his gruff tone grudging. "Dr. Montague had information that could get the bad cop fired and put in jail."

"I know in my gut that this dirty cop killed Henry," said Beanie. "There is no other better suspect."

"What about the mystery guy in the hoodie you told us about?" asked Sophie. "The one Green saw on the clinic surveillance video he accidentally erased."

"Green likes him as a suspect," said Beanie. "He thinks the guy might be PC-5, but I'm not sure."

"He's the mystery guy your sister saw with Henry, right?" Asked Sophie.

Beanie nodded. "He gave Henry an envelope of cash."

"And why do you suppose he did that?" asked Caleb. "Might have been an extortion payment."

"What if Dr. Montague was blackmailing the mystery guy?" asked Sophie. "That would give him a motive."

Beanie nodded. "True, but ..."

Caleb said, "But think about this—Detective Green may have seen the mystery guy at Dr. Adams' clinic. So, what was he doing there?"

Sophie said, "Dr. Adams, Dr. Montague, and the mystery guy might have been mixed up in some scam."

"Detective Green suggested that," said Beanie. "And when I suggested it to Octavia and Robyn, they thought it might be possible, but—"

Beanie's cell phone rang, and he glanced at the Caller-ID. "It's Stevie ... "

Sophie said, "Ask him if his cousin was able to hack Dr. Montague's laptop."

Answering, Beanie said, "Hey, what's up?"

"I'm heading to the office," said Stevie. "And guess what I have?"

"What?" asked Beanie.

"Dr. Montague's laptop," announced Stevie. "My cousin figured out the password."

"Thank God," said Beanie, flooded with relief. "What time will you be here?"

"About a half an hour," said Stevie.

"See you then," said Beanie. After ending the call, he updated Sophie and Caleb.

Sophie said, "We might be about to find out the identity of Henry's killer."

Beanie said, "I need to call Detective Green."

"Why?" asked Caleb.

"Because Henry's killer is probably the dirty cop," said Beanie. "Green needs to know so he can call his PIIB contact. Two birds are about to be killed with one stone. Henry's killer will be arrested and a bad cop will no longer have a foothold in the St. Killian police department."

39

"Where's Stevie?" asked Sophie, poking her head into Beanie's cubicle.

Beanie glanced at his watch. "That's what I'd like to know…"

Three hours had passed since Stevie called to tell Beanie that his cousin had successfully hacked Henry's laptop. Beanie had been on pins and needles, waiting for Stevie to arrive, anxious to discover the identity of Henry's killer. But after thirty minutes came and went, Beanie figured Stevie had been delayed by traffic. When an hour had gone by, Beanie suspected that Stevie had incorrectly estimated his time of arrival. Now, he was starting to think Stevie had become distracted by some last-minute detour he'd had to make.

"He should have been here by now," said Sophie.

Beanie nodded. "Hours ago."

Wandering into the cubicle, Sophie dropped down into the chair in front of Beanie's desk. "You should call him."

"I am," said Beanie. "I was going to an hour ago, but Vivian sent some revisions to one of my stories, so—"

Beanie's desk phone rang. "One second," he told Sophie, then answered the phone.

"Hey, it's Stevie …"

"Where are you?" asked Beanie, mouthing to Sophie that Stevie was on the line when she gave him a questioning glance.

"Where is he?" demanded Sophie.

"I'm at the police station," said Stevie.

"The police station?" echoed Beanie.

"What is he doing at the police station?" Sophie asked. "Put him on speaker."

"Hey, Sophie's here with me," said Beanie. "I'm going to put you on speaker."

His disembodied voice filling the small cubicle, Stevie said, "I was headed to the office, driving along the coastal road, when I got carjacked."

Sophie gasped. "Carjacked?"

"What?" demanded Beanie.

"Somebody carjacked you?" asked Sophie.

"Why do you sound surprised?" asked Stevie. "I was driving the Lambo."

Beanie was confused. "Lambo?"

Sophie rolled her eyes. "He means that ridiculous Lamborghini."

"Ridiculous Lamborghini," said Stevie, clearly offended. "How can an innovative masterpiece of Italian engineering be ridiculous?"

"Innovative masterpiece of Italian engineering?" Sophie scoffed. "Did you really just say that?"

"Not only did I say it," said Stevie. "But I also meant it."

"You guys, please …" interjected Beanie. His little boys didn't bicker as much as Sophie and Stevie argued. His co-workers were notorious for debating the most nonsensical, nonessential nonsense. "Stevie, tell us what happened to you."

"As I said, I was heading to the office," began Stevie. "I was driving along the coastal road when I noticed this car driving up fast behind me. Next thing I know, the car slammed me from behind. I was forced off the road. After I got out of my car, the guy runs up to me and he's got a gun in my face."

"Oh my God!"

Beanie was shocked. "He pulled a gun on you?"

"He demanded the Lambo," said Stevie. "So, I gave it to him, you know, so I wouldn't get shot in the face. But the good thing is, I have other Lambos."

Sophie scoffed. "Did you really just say that?"

Stevie said, "Oh, and I got a good look at the guy who took my car. I've been at the police station for the last two hours working with a sketch artist.."

Beanie said, "That's good news. Hopefully, they'll catch the guy."

Stevie said, "Yeah, but there's bad news, too …"

"What's the bad news?" asked Sophie.

"Dr. Montague's laptop was in the car," said Stevie. "I'm sorry, but it's gone …"

40

"All is not lost," said Octavia, seated at the head of the long, oblong table in the conference room she'd booked at the Queen Palm, where she was staying, for the strategy session regarding Robyn's case.

A week had passed since Stevie's expensive Italian sports car—and Henry's laptop—had been stolen.

"How can you say that?" asked Robyn, pacing in front of the wall of French doors overlooking lush, tropical landscaping. "We don't have the laptop and from what Detective Green told Beanie, we're not going to get it back!"

Exhaling, Beanie recalled his conversation with the detective. Green had doubted Henry's laptop would be found, and even if it was, all the data on the device would have been wiped. Beanie figured that by now, the laptop was in some pawn shop, its files deleted.

"We may not have Henry's laptop but we have surveillance video from Henry's townhouse the night he died," said Octavia.

"That video does more to hurt me than help me," said Robyn, shaking her head.

Nodding, Beanie said, "It shows Robyn and Henry arguing in the breezeway. Then Henry leaves. Robyn goes back to the townhouse, then leaves the townhouse. An hour later, Robyn returns. Henry doesn't."

"Janvier thinks Henry didn't come back because I shot him." Arms folded tightly across her chest, Robyn's pacing increased, her wedge heels pounding the stamped carpet. "Which isn't true. Not really. I mean, yes, I shot at Henry that night, but ...."

"There is another video," said Octavia.

Confused, Beanie asked, "There is? When Detective Green showed me that video, he said there was nothing else on it after around ten that night."

"I'm talking about a surveillance video of that night from a different angle," said Octavia. "Unlike the video Green showed you, Beanie, the second video recorded a twenty-four-hour period, from eight in the morning until eight the following morning."

Beanie said, "Green mentioned that video ..."

"I remember that," said Robyn. "That was the day Janvier came to the townhouse with the search warrant."

"I've requested that the St. Killian Police Department produce the video," said Octavia. "So far, Janvier has dragged his feet, but I'll get the surveillance from the security company that monitors the complex if I have to. Until we can get the second video and take a look at it, we need to focus on our list of better suspects."

"What better suspects?" Robyn scoffed. "Mimi has an alibi for the night Henry died. Liz Adams is dead."

"Don't forget about the PC-5," said Octavia. "Henry might not be so lovey-dovey with the cartel, after all."

"Lime Shoes said there was no beef between Henry and the PC-5," reminded Beanie. "Their arrangement was working fine. It was beneficial for both parties."

"Until maybe it wasn't," said Octavia. "The cartel should stay on the list of better suspects. Lime Shoes is not the only source at our disposal. My cousin Icarus has a few associates in the cartel he can talk to."

Beanie said, "We can't forget about the mystery guy in the hoodie."

"The guy who gave Henry the envelope full of cash," said Robyn.

"Detective Green likes him for Dr. Liz Adams' murder," said Octavia.

"But how are we supposed to find this guy?" asked Robyn. "No one even knows what the guy really looks like."

Octavia said, "We might have to let the cops do their jobs and find the guy. In the meantime, I'd like to focus on Henry's other blackmail victim. Not Dr. Taylor. I'm talking about Magenta Flower."

The name Magenta Flower sent a jolt through Beanie. Where had he heard the name before?

"Henry sent emails to that Magenta Flower email address," said Robyn.

Octavia consulted her notes. "But, according to the emails, Magenta Flower didn't have much money to give Henry, but he did give him a Rolex."

"Which I'm pretty sure Henry sold," said Robyn.

Octavia said, "If we can trace the sale—"

"How could we do that?" Robyn cut in.

"You don't take a six-figure watch down to the local pawn dealer," said Octavia. "I'm sure Henry went to an independent jeweler and—"

"I think Henry was emailing the dirty cop," said Beanie.

Robyn asked, "What makes you think that?"

"Lime Shoes," said Beanie, recalling the conversation with the old gangster.

Octavia tilted her head. "Lime Shoes told you that Henry emailed the dirty cop?"

"No, no, I meant …" Beanie rubbed his jaw. "Lime Shoes told me that the dirty cop was called Mag Flo."

"And … so?" Robyn demanded.

"Mag … Flo …" said Beanie, hoping to make his sister and Octavia understand, though he wasn't quite sure of his theory himself. "Mag … for Magenta. Flo … for Flower. Mag Flo could be Magenta Flower. Which means Henry was blackmailing the dirty cop."

Robyn shook her head. "Seems like a stretch to me."

Octavia said, "I don't think so. Beanie might be right."

Robyn said, "Then we just need to get the dirty cop's name from the email Henry sent him and we can tell Janvier."

"I found the email," said Octavia. "Unfortunately, the name is just … magenta flower at island mail dot com."

"Maybe we could trace the Magenta Flower email address," suggested Robyn.

"That might take too long," said Beanie, anxious to share his thoughts. "And the trace might lead to a dead end. Anyone can create an email address from anywhere in the world. I have a better idea. We can set a trap for the dirty cop."

"What kind of trap?" asked Robyn, skepticism in her narrowed gaze.

Beanie said, "If the dirty cop killed Henry, then there must have been proof of that in the files on Henry's laptop. Now, I'm guessing the dirty cop doesn't know about the evidence on the laptop. So, I'm thinking we could send a message to magenta flower. We can say we have evidence that proves he—or she—is a dirty cop."

"We tell the dirty cop he can have the evidence—for a price," said Robyn.

"Exactly," said Beanie. "Then we set up a meeting to exchange the evidence for the money and—"

Octavia said, "I don't like this idea. It's dangerous. And you don't know for sure that magenta flower is the dirty cop."

Beanie said, "It will be risky."

"But it's a risk I think I have to take," said Robyn.

Octavia pinched the bridge of her nose. "I don't like it, but …"

Beanie said, "But I think we have to try. I'll email magenta flower, and let you know what happens."

41

"I can't believe the dirty cop contacted you," said Robyn.

"To tell you the truth," said Beanie, using the Bluetooth in his SUV to talk with his sister. "I can't either. I was shocked, even though I'd been hoping he'd email me."

Three days ago,

After pitching his idea of trapping the mole to Octavia and Robyn, Beanie had sent an email to the Magenta Flower address. *There is video evidence that implicates you in the murder of Dr. Henry Montague. I will give it to you, but it will cost you.* There had been no response. Beanie struggled to contain his disappointment and frustration. The next day, Beanie had monitored his email account as he went about his day. Between fact-checking articles, covering crime stories, and interviewing witnesses, he'd waited for a message from Magenta Flower, or rather, Mag Flo, the bad cop. But there had been no contact.

Driving into work this morning, Beanie had doubts that his plan would work. Maybe he'd been naïve. Maybe Mag Flo hadn't taken him seriously. Maybe the email account had been suspended. Or maybe Mag Flo no longer checked that particular account. That would make sense. Mag Flo wouldn't want any digital trace of his connection to Henry.

As Beanie had been in the breakroom getting his third cup of coffee of the day, he'd received an email alert.

Back at his desk, he accessed his personal email account.

Heart thudding, he'd stared at the message from Magenta Flower: *who are you?* Stunned, his hands shaking, Beanie typed a reply: *Don't worry about who I am ... worry about the evidence I have that can send you to jail for the rest of your life.* Several minutes later, Magenta Flower responded: *How much do you want for the evidence?* With trembling fingers, Beanie replied: *A thousand dollars.* Five minutes later, Magenta Flower replied: *Where can we meet?* Beanie typed: *Adagio Bay mall 7 pm. At the Cup-O-Joe coffee shop.* Magenta Flower replied: *How will I know who you are?* Beanie responded: *I'll be wearing a Palmchat Islanders t-shirt.*

Beanie had called Robyn after the email exchanges with Magenta Flower.

"What time are you meeting him again?" asked Robyn.

Checking his watch, Beanie said, "Seven. The dirty cop should be here in fifteen minutes."

Robyn asked, "You have the evidence you're going to exchange?"

Beanie reached into his pocket and pulled out the small thumb drive. "Got it right here."

"And what's on it?" asked Robyn. "I'm sure he'll ask. He might even want to take a look before he gives you the money."

Beanie said, "I'm going to tell him it's video of him talking to Henry about being a dirty cop. But—"

"But what if he wants to see the evidence, Roland?" asked Robyn.

Noticing the tension in his sister's tone, Beanie tried to calm her nerves. "The point is not really to exchange information for money. I need to find out who this crooked cop is, so I can tell Detective Green. I'm thinking of trying to use the record app on my phone to get audio of our conversation. I'm hoping to get him to say his name, or—"

"Hey, can you hold on a second," interrupted Robyn. "Actually, I need to call you back. I'm being called to the ER."

"Okay, yeah, that's fine."

"Roland, be careful, please."

"You know I will."

"Don't do anything stupid," warned Robyn. "And don't take any unnecessary chances. If things start to go sideways, promise me you'll walk away."

Ending the call with Robyn, Beanie glanced around. He inhaled, then exhaled, trying to calm his nerves and his chaotic thoughts. It was hard to fathom that he was about to meet the person who might have murdered Henry. He wasn't anxious to come face to face with a cold-blooded killer but discovering the identity of the dirty cop made the risks worth it.

Still, Robyn's concerns worried him.

Disturbed by the idea of the situation going south, Beanie struggled to swallow his fear. Anxiousness and apprehension were normal. But there was no need for terror. He doubted Mag Flo would try anything crazy in public. The outdoor mall teemed with tourists and residents, shopping and browsing as they traversed the pedestrian walkways.

Still, Beanie worried something would go wrong. What if Mag Flo demanded to see the evidence, as Robyn had suggested he might? What would Beanie do then? What could he do except stall and stammer? There was nothing on the thumb drive other than a few fake video files of stock footage he'd downloaded from the Internet. He hoped to convince Mag Flo that the drive contained damaging evidence. But, if the dirty cop called his bluff, then—

"You got something for me?"

Beanie glanced up. Across from him, a gangly guy in a dark hoodie, sunglasses, and a baseball cap sat in the chair. The guy sniffed, dragging a finger beneath his nose as his head whipped left and right.

His heart pounding, Beanie let out a low breath. Mag Flo was sitting in front of him. The man who might have killed Henry twitched, his micro-movements furtive and suspicious. Again, he sniffed and used the cuff of his sleeve to wipe his nose.

Beanie frowned. Something about the guy seemed off. Wrong. Was the guy really a cop? He couldn't imagine the man working for the St. Killian police department.

"Where's what you got?" he demanded. "I ain't got all night."

"Yeah, I got it," said Beanie, confusion replacing his apprehension. For some reason, the emaciated guy with the runny nose didn't look like a killer.

Not that killers had a certain look. From his years covering crime, Beanie had seen all types of murderers. Anyone could put a bullet between someone's eyes under the wrong circumstances. Still, there was something … marginalized and disenfranchised about the guy. He reminded Beanie of one of those Handweg deadbeats who congregated on front porches and around liquor stores, doing everything except looking for gainful employment.

Mag Flo didn't look like a cop, and he didn't seem like the kind of guy Henry would have chosen as a partner to run scams with. But, again, Beanie cautioned himself not to judge on appearances. Scam artists didn't have a specific look.

"We gonna do this deal, or not?"

Beanie nodded. "You have the money?"

"Let me see what you got first," demanded Mag Flo.

"It's on a jump drive," said Beanie, holding the device between his thumb and index finger. "It's—"

Mag Flo karate chopped Beanie's wrist.

The thumb drive dropped to the table as Beanie cried out in pain and astonishment. Mag Flo swiped the jump drive, leaped up, pivoted, and took off running. Flabbergasted, Beanie stared at the crooked cop, sprinting away, weaving in and out of the meandering crowd, some of whom he pushed and shoved in his effort to get away. Recovering from shock and embarrassment, Beanie took off after Mag Flo. Keeping the dirty cop in sight, Beanie followed him. Ten minutes later, Mag Flo turned down a short alleyway. Beanie followed suit. The alley ended in an alcove where restrooms were located. As the crooked cop barreled into the men's room, Beanie slowed to a stop near a large bougainvillea bush in a giant ceramic planter. He took out his phone and sent a group text to Robyn and Octavia.

I met with the dirty cop at the Adagio Bay outdoor mall... he stole the fake jump drive then ran into the men's room near the Ralph Lauren store ... call the police ...

Several seconds later, Robyn texted: *ok and be careful! Don't be a hero.*

Octavia responded: *I'm calling Detective Janvier right now!*

Beanie frowned. Now, what did he do? Stand outside the men's room holding his phone? He thought of calling the cops himself, but Octavia was taking care of alerting Janvier.

Pocketing his phone, Beanie walked to the men's room door. Wrapping his hand around the knob, he twisted it slowly and pushed the door open. Beanie slipped into the restroom's foyer, a small area occupied by a trash can and a paper towel dispenser. Around the corner, where the urinals and stalls were, Beanie heard conversation.

Pausing near the trash can, Beanie listened.

"Now, hit me over the head, Willie."

A chill passed through Beanie. The voice was familiar. It was Detective Allan Green. Beanie was confused. Had Octavia called Green instead? Had the detective gotten to the men's room so quickly because he'd been in the area, or—

No, that didn't make sense. Beanie reflected on what Green had said. *Hit me over the head, Willie.*

"Why I got to do that?"

Beanie recognized the voice as the guy who'd karate chopped his wrist before running off with the jump drive. It was the guy he'd assumed was Mag Flo, the dirty cop. But Green had called the guy Willie. Beanie was confused. So did that mean the guy wasn't the dirty cop? If so, why had he shown up pretending to be Mag Flo? And if the guy wasn't the bad cop, if he was someone named Willie, then who was Mag Flo?

"We need to make it look like you knocked me out and got away with the evidence … "

Beanie frowned. What was going on? Why was Detective Green talking to the dirty cop? Why was he telling Willie to knock him out and get away with the evidence?

Green said, "Don't hit me too hard but make it look good …"

"What happens after I hit you?"

"I'll call for backup and tell them you're in the wind," said Green. "Then I'll text you so we can meet up and you can give me the evidence."

A hard knot dropped into Beanie's stomach.

Willie said, "And you can give me my money."

"Yeah, right … "

"So what's on this jump drive?" asked Willie. "What's the evidence against you?"

"That stupid reporter says it's video of me talking to Henry Montague."

Willie asked, "Who's Henry Montague?"

"Mob doctor," said Green. "The guy found dead near the marina."

"You killed that doctor?" asked the mole.

"Didn't have a choice," said Green. "He was blackmailing me."

"Blackmailing you?"

"He threatened to tell my superiors about some scams me and him ran together," said Green. "He could have gotten me arrested."

Trembling with fear and anger, Beanie turned toward the men's room door. His heart felt like a jackhammer in his chest. He couldn't believe what he'd heard. Detective Green had killed Henry? Green was Magenta Flower? Mag Flo, the dirty cop? How could that be? Didn't make any sense. How could Green be the crooked cop who'd killed Henry? The detective had been a staunch and supportive ally since Robyn had been arrested for Henry's murder. Even before then, Green had promised to help clear Robyn's name. He'd agreed that Detective Janvier was on the wrong track. When Janvier had refused to provide Beanie with any information about Robyn's case, Green had provided crucial updates. Beanie was floored. Green had been lying all this time. Making a fool of him. How could he have missed the signs of Green's treachery?

Shaking the negative thoughts away, Beanie grabbed the door handle, and—

"Freeze Beanie … "

Detective Green's cold, calculated voice sent an icy jolt through Beanie.

"Don't take another step," commanded Green. "Don't make me shoot you in the back."

With a resigned exhale, Beanie turned and raised his hands.

"What are you doing in here?" asked Green.

"I could ask you the same thing," said Beanie, unable to hide his contempt. "Except I doubt you'd tell me the truth. I wouldn't expect a dirty cop to be honest."

"Watch the insults," warned Green. "This dirty cop tried to help your sister."

It was Beanie's turn to scoff. "You tried to help? How?"

Green's smirk was smug. "Well, for one, I didn't tell Janvier that your sister lied to him."

"My sister didn't—"

"Yeah, she did," insisted Green. "Which I'm sure you know. Robyn didn't tell Janvier that she confronted Henry in the dunes behind the townhouse complex. Didn't tell him that Henry dumped her, so she shot at him. Yeah, I was there. Saw everything. But I said nothing to Janvier. So, yeah, I did help your sister."

Angered by Green's faulty logic, Beanie asked, "Why were you there?"

"Henry and I were going to meet on the beach," said Green. "Have a conversation about his ridiculous blackmail demands. Henry was late—due to his little lovers' quarrel with your sister—so I headed up through the dunes toward the townhouse. As I said, I was there."

"So you met with Henry," said Beanie. "You shot him. How did you get his gun?"

"After Robyn fired those warning shots," began Green, "I started to think of how I could turn the situation around to my advantage. I followed your sister back to the townhouse. She went through the front door, but I slipped into the terrace doors, which were open."

"And then what?" asked Beanie, his heart slamming, terrified, and infuriated that Green had slipped into the townhouse without Robyn's knowledge.

"Your sister put the gun into the nightstand drawer," said Green. "Then she went into the bathroom and took a shower."

"So you got the gun," said Beanie, stunned by Green's revelations.

"After that, I jogged back to the dunes," said Green. "I saw Henry in the dunes, with his back to me, and then I just decided to get rid of him right then and there."

Beanie shook his head at Green's calculated callousness. "You shot him in the back."

"He had it coming," said Green, shrugging.

"He died thinking my sister shot him," said Beanie.

Willie cursed under his breath. "That's cold-blooded, man."

"You think I'm cold-blooded, Willie?" Green glared at Willie. "Henry was worse. I told him I was done doing scams with him. He was getting bolder and I couldn't take the risk of getting caught. That's when he decided to blackmail me to keep getting money. Squeezed me for every dime I had.

They might as well have put his name on my paychecks. One time, when I couldn't pay him, he took my Rolex."

"Your Rolex?" Beanie thought of the emails between Henry and Magenta Flower.

His expression injured, Green said, "Henry forced me to give it to him. That Rolex was a gift from my grandfather. When I went back to the townhouse to return the gun to the drawer, I decided to look around for it. While I was looking around, I knocked over a vase. Robyn must have heard me because I hear her call out Henry's name. Next thing I know, she's coming into the living room just as I jump out through the terrace doors."

"She thought you were a shadow," said Beanie, realizing Robyn's initial beliefs about an intruder had been right.

Green said, "Or maybe she was hoping to finish what she'd started."

"Robyn didn't want Henry dead," said Beanie. "She was just trying to scare him when she shot at him."

"Well, when Willie shoots at you," said Green. "It's not going to be to scare you. It's going to be to kill you." Willie shook his head. "You didn't say I had to shoot nobody."

Green sighed. "You're not."

Frowning, Willie said, "But you just said—"

"You're not going to shoot him," said Green. "I'm going to do the honors."

"You don't have to kill me," said Beanie, thinking fast. "In fact, you shouldn't."

Green's eyes narrowed. "And why is that? The way I see it, I have to kill you. Not only do you know that I killed Henry, but you know I'm dirty."

Beanie said, "If you kill me, you won't be able to destroy the evidence against you."

"What are you talking about?" asked Green.

"There's nothing on that jump drive your friend took from me," said Beanie.

Glancing at the sniffling guy, Beanie detected an uneasy suspicion in his expression as he gave Green a side-eyed glare.

Green frowned. "What?"

"There is nothing on that thumb drive except useless stock footage."

"Where is the real evidence?" Green demanded.

"It's on Henry's laptop," said Beanie.

Green barked a harsh laugh. "Try again. The laptop was stolen from that rich brat's stupid sports car. Which, actually, helped me out quite a bit."

"How so?" asked Beanie.

"Well, once the laptop was stolen, I didn't have to worry about those files coming back to haunt me. I didn't have to worry about trying to get it from your sister like I tried to get it from Dr. Adams," said Green. "The good doctor claimed she didn't have it or know where it was. Not that I believed her."

"So you killed her?" asked Beanie.

Green shrugged. "Henry had files on that laptop that incriminated me."

"Files that identified you as his killer?" asked Beanie.

"Files that gave me the strongest motive for murder," admitted Green. "Dr. Adams might have taken a look at those files. When she begged me not to kill her, she swore she hadn't looked at any of the files. But when someone's life is on the line, they'll say anything to stay alive."

Catching Green's subtle threat, Beanie swallowed. "Look, the laptop may have been stolen, but the files aren't gone. Stevie's hacker cousin made backup copies. I can get those files for you, but you have to let me go."

Green shook his head. "You're not going anywhere. But you are going to give me the laptop files—if they even exist."

Beanie fought panic. "The files exist. But you have to let me go so I can get them."

"Tell me exactly where the files are," said Green. "Willie will get them."

"Man, I don't have time to run no errands," complained Willie. "You ain't say nothing about going to get no laptop files."

"Well, I am saying it now," said Green, taking a few steps backward, angling his body to swing the gun from Beanie to Willie. "You're going to get the laptop and—"

Willie karate chopped Green's wrist.

The lightning-quick move startled Beanie, and Green, who wailed in shock and pain as the gun dropped to the floor and clattered across the tiles toward the door.

Beanie lunged for the gun, but Willie shoved him into the wall, picked up the gun, and dashed out of the men's room. Wincing and holding his injured wrist, Green cursed as he lurched toward Beanie. Deciding to throw a punch, Beanie raised his fist as Green stumbled forward and—

The men's room door burst open.

"Freeze! Don't move!" came the shouts and commands from the half dozen St. Killian police officers who rushed into the men's room.

EPILOGUE

"I can't believe that Detective Green is the dirty cop who killed Henry," said Robyn, shaking her head.

Sitting next to his sister, Beanie lounged in the Adirondack chair on the backyard patio.

Soca music, balloon arches, and flags strung between palm trees fluttered in the late afternoon breeze as Beanie glanced around the backyard. Dozens of family and friends milled about, mingling, talking, eating, laughing, and dancing.

The festive atmosphere was infectious and engaging, much like the 30th birthday had been weeks ago. Once again, Noelle had planned a gathering to celebrate the St. Killian police department's decision to officially drop all charges against Robyn for the murders of Dr. Henry Montague and Dr. Liz Adams. Several feet away, Noelle chased Ethan and Evan through the freshly mowed grass, laughing as the boys squealed with excitement.

"Neither can I," said Beanie, taking a sip of his Felipe beer, enjoying the balmy afternoon breeze blowing through the palm trees. "When I think about it …"

"How did we miss the signs?" asked Robyn. "Were there any signs? Green was so compassionate and supportive. He was always sharing information and doing whatever he could to make sure Janvier didn't railroad me."

"Green fooled everybody," said Beanie, smiling as his parents, Noelle, and a few of his cousins chased Ethan, Evan, and the other kids through the freshly mowed grass, laughing as the children squealed with excitement.

"And he was going to kill you," said Robyn.

"But he didn't," Beanie reminded her, not in the mood to relive the harrowing incident, still fresh in his memory more than a week later.

After the cops swarmed into the men's room, Detective Green tried to convince Detective Janvier and the group of officers that he had been apprehending a suspect when Beanie had accidentally wandered into the bathroom. Green's lie was immediately disputed by Beanie, and Willie, who'd realized Green was trying to throw him under the bus.

Soon, Beanie found himself fighting to be heard over both Green and Willie until Janvier ordered everyone to shut up. Next thing Beanie knew, he, Green, and Willie were in the back of squad cars heading to the St. Killian police station.

"You could have died because of me," said Robyn, her expression pained. "Because of my stupid decisions. I hooked up with a blackmailing psycho. And why? Because I was turning thirty and I was still single and wanted a husband so bad that it didn't matter what kind of person he was."

Beanie recalled the conversation he'd had with Dr. Liz Adams about women compromising their standards for the sake of marriage and a family. Beanie hated the idea of his sister thinking she had to settle for a bum like Henry.

Robyn said, "So what's going to happen to Green? Is he going to Tiverton for the rest of his life?"

"Most likely, considering all the evidence against him," said Beanie. "Not only that but, in addition to my statement against Green, Willie also agreed to flip on him."

Robyn frowned. "Are your statements going to be enough to keep Green in jail? What if he says it's your word against his?"

"He's already saying that," said Beanie. "He's claiming he's being set up and that the police department is conspiring against him. But—and here's something you won't believe—we may have to rethink our assessment of Janvier's detective abilities."

"Why would we want to do that?"

Beanie sighed. "Turns out, after Green accidentally on purpose erased the video, Janvier put a secret tail on him."

Robyn's eyes narrowed. "A secret tail?"

"Janvier was hoping to find evidence that Green was destroying evidence on your behalf."

Robyn shook her head. "Ridiculous."

"Instead, Janvier found out that Green was shaking down low-level PC-5 members, stealing money and drugs from his collars. Remember the mystery guy in the hoodie?"

"The one who gave Henry the envelope of cash," said Robyn, nodding.

"He was Green's partner," said Beanie. "Janvier nabbed him and convinced him to flip on Green, too. Turns out, the mystery hoodie guy knew that Green had killed Henry."

"Does mystery hoodie guy know that Green killed Liz Adams?"

Beanie scratched his chin. "Not sure about that. But, both Willie and I gave statements swearing we heard Green admit to killing her."

Robyn sighed. "God. Liz is dead because of me, too."

"Robyn ..." admonished Beanie. "Don't say that."

"But—"

"No, buts, okay?" said Beanie. "None of Green's crimes are your fault. He chose to be a dirty cop. He chose to kill people. And he chose to try to cover his tracks, but he didn't get away with it."

"I know that," said Robyn. "But, still ... it scares me to think that I could have gone to jail for murder."

"But, you didn't," said Beanie reaching to grab his sister's hand. "I always knew you were innocent. I knew you couldn't have killed anybody."

"Even though Henry said I'd shot him?"

Beanie squeezed Robyn's hand. "Henry didn't know the truth."

"Which is so sad," said Robyn. "He died thinking I'd tried to kill him. I never should have shot at him. Why was I trying to scare him? What did I think that would accomplish? What was I thinking?"

"I know it's tough," said Beanie. "But ... I know that one day, as time passes, you'll find a way to forgive yourself. And you'll also realize that Henry wasn't the right guy for you. I mean, not to speak ill of the dead, but the guy wasn't faithful. He blackmailed people. Worked for the mob."

Robyn said, "He still didn't deserve to be shot in the back like a dog."

Beanie exhaled. He wasn't quite sure what to say. Wasn't quite sure how to make his sister feel better, but he supposed she wasn't holding him responsible for lifting her spirits. It would take time for her to come to terms with the tragic ending of her relationship with Dr. Henry Montague. Beanie figured the best thing he could do was offer support and sympathy when Robyn needed it.

As a jaunty calypso song filled the air, Noelle called to Beanie and Robyn to join the celebration. Several feet away, guests laughed as they got in position to participate in the line dance associated with the song.

"Come on," said Beanie, pulling Robyn to her feet. "Let's show these people how to do the dance."

Laughing, Robyn said, "Let's hope I remember the steps!"

***

Did you think Roland "Beanie" Bean's sister Robyn had killed her boyfriend?

I'm sure she seemed very suspicious, and her evasive half-truths didn't help her case, so it was a good thing that she had a super sleuth brother to figure things out and keep her out of prison!

As an investigative reporter, Beanie always finds himself dealing with a dead body, especially around a holiday—and Easter is no exception.

In *Easter Egg Hunt Murder*, Beanie and his young son Evan are hunting for eggs when they stumble upon a sleeping lady beneath the bushes at an Easter egg hunt party. Beanie knows the truth though. The woman isn't sleeping, she's dead. As he covers the story, he realizes that the killer is a lot closer to home and willing to do whatever it takes from being discovered.

If you love holiday cozy murder mysteries with plenty of twists and turns to keep you guessing until the shocking ending, then grab Easter Egg Hunt Murder today!

Are you eagerly anticipating Beanie's next unexpected detour into a mystery waiting to be solved?

Then **Beanie's Mini Mystery Moments** are for you!

Get an exclusive quick-read mystery that spins off from one of Beanie's mystery adventures delivered straight to your email inbox!
https://BookHip.com/SAZTBNW

ALSO BY RACHEL WOODS

SASSY SARCASTIC CAT COZY MYSTERIES

Sophie Carter, a struggling reporter for the *Palmchat Gazette*, teams up with a sassy talking Calico cat to solve crimes as she strives to become an influential investigative reporter

A SLY AND SINISTER TAIL

A COLD AND CALCULATING TAIL

A FOUL AND FRIGHTENING TAIL

A DARK AND DEVIOUS TAIL

REPORTER ROLAND BEAN COZY MYSTERIES

Roland "Beanie" Bean, husband and loving father, finds himself the unwitting participant in solving crimes as he seeks to make a name for himself as a reporter for the *Palmchat Gazette.*

HAPPY BIRTHDAY MURDER

EASTER EGG HUNT MURDER

MERRY CHRISTMAS MURDER

TRICK OR TREAT MURDER

GOBBLE GOBBLE MURDER

HAPPY 4TH OF JULY MURDER

SUMMER VACATION MURDER

HAPPY NEW YEAR MURDER

PALMCHAT ISLANDS MYSTERIES

Married journalists, Vivian and Leo, manage the island newspaper while solving crimes as they chase leads for their next story.

UNTIL DEATH DO US PART

NO ONE WILL FIND YOU

YOU WILL DIE FOR THIS

DON'T MAKE ME HURT YOU

THE PALMCHAT ISLANDS MYSTERIES BOX SET: BOOKS 1 - 4

RUTHLESS REVENGE ROMANCE SERIES

Gripping romantic suspense series with steamy romance, unpredictable plot twists and devastating consequences of deceit.

HER DEADLY MISTAKE

HER DEADLY DECEPTION

HER DEADLY THREAT

HER DEADLY BETRAYAL

MURDER IN PARADISE SERIES

A series of stand-alone women sleuth mysteries with murder, mayhem and a dash of romance, set against the backdrop of turquoise waters and swaying palm trees of the fictional Palmchat Islands.

THE UNWORTHY WIFE

THE SILENT ENEMY

THE PERFECT LIAR

ABOUT THE AUTHOR

Rachel Woods studied journalism and graduated from the University of Houston where she published articles in the Daily Cougar. She is a legal assistant by day and a freelance writer and blogger with a penchant for melodrama by night. Many of her stories take place on the islands, which she has visited around the world. Rachel resides in Houston, Texas with her three sock monkeys.

For more information:
www.therachelwoods.com
rachel@therachelwoods.com

ABOUT THE PUBLISHER

BONZAIMOON BOOKS

BonzaiMoon Books is a family-run, artisanal publishing company created in the summer of 2014. We publish works of fiction in various genres. Our passion and focus is working with authors who write the books you want to read, and giving those authors the opportunity to have more direct input in the publishing of their work.

For more information:
www.bonzaimoonbooks.com
info@bonzaimoonbooks.com